Summer People

by

Corinne LaBalme

Summer People

COPYRIGHT © 2022 by Corinne LaBalme

Cover Art by *Diana Carlile*

The Wild Rose Press, Inc.
PO Box 708
Adams Basin, NY 14410-0708
Visit us at www.thewildrosepress.com

Publishing History
First Edition, 2022
Trade Paperback ISBN 978-1-5092-4327-3
Digital ISBN 978-1-5092-4328-0

Published in the United States of America

"Rick, this is tremendous!" exclaimed Jessica, staring at her plate. "It looks like something out of a magazine."

"So do you," thought Rick, watching the candlelight throw its sparkling glow across Jessica's face as they sat down. Time to put Plan A into gear. Time to tell her how much I'm looking forward to meeting this husband of hers. That called for a toast, didn't it? He raised his glass.

"To you…" he began.

Jessica leaned forward, both hands cupping her wineglass.

"To you and…" Wait a second! Where was that humongous gem she had on her left-hand ring finger this morning? What kind of crazy game was this woman playing with him?

"Yes…?" prompted Jessica.

"To you…and to the unexpected," said Rick slowly.

Dedication

To Harriet Stratemeyer Adams (AKA Carolyn Keene)
who taught me how to play bridge without 'tells' and
that any story, any time, works best when it's served up
with a smattering of mystery…

Acknowledgements

I'd like to thank the 'real' Kim Adams, Chris Bart, Roger Conover, John Curtin, Mark Depman, George Ellenbogen, Polly Ford, Dan Kelly, Shauna Kelly, Earl McMillin, Lois and Bill Racz, Chris Vogel (and not to forget Nancy and Melanie) for the good memories, their friendship over the years, and the much appreciated 'loan' of their excellent names.

Chapter One

"State your needs clearly! Use the negotiating skills we learned in Lesson Three…"

Jessica punched the mute button in irritation. What if you explained exactly what you wanted, and got frozen out before the discussion got started?

Three weeks on Cape Cod.

That was all she'd asked for. Three weeks in the antique house that she'd discovered as a dilapidated ruin and lovingly restored into a white clapboard dream-house, the house that was featured last year in the *Cape Cod Times* as one of the area's "Ten Prettiest Vacation Properties."

Honestly? She'd have settled for two weeks.

Instead, once again, she'd be handing the keys over to the rental agent. Perfect strangers would be sipping iced tea on the wrought iron picnic table in "her" back lawn on hot summer days. They'd be curling up on "her" Victorian love seat with a good book on quiet afternoons and sleeping soundly under the lacy canopy of "her" four-poster bed. Jessica was suffering from a chronic case of real estate envy, and the droning voice of the guru on the self-help CD doing wasn't doing much to alleviate it. He just spouted a lot of happy-snappy chit-chat about "visualizing the obstacles in your path" and "harnessing your will-power to make negative forces disintegrate."

Jessica grinned as she put her foot on the accelerator and sped past the camper that had been ambling down the Mid-Cape highway at roughly thirty miles below the speed limit. If only all obstacles in her path could shift so neatly to the rear-view mirror.

She didn't want Max to disintegrate…but his attitudes certainly did qualify as a negative force in her life, specifically when they affected the Cape Cod cottage. Her husband's concepts of "home" and "vacation" had been set in stone during his privileged Boston childhood. The family's posh, six-bedroom Back Bay mansion fit his "home" specifications nicely while five-star European hotels with fancy restaurants, in-house spas and room service took care of the "vacation" category.

Jessica had never developed a fondness for the luxury resorts her husband favored. The way the snooty concierge in Monte Carlo had snickered at her French-Canadian accent still stung—and having a waiter in black-tie hovering over you at the swimming pool took some of the fun out of sunbathing. Without consulting her, Max made reservations for August at the super elegant Hotel Cipriani in Venice. It was downright ridiculous to cringe about the prospect of four weeks at one of the world's showiest resorts, but frankly she'd trade a whole fleet of golden gondolas for a ride in a beat-up Boston Whaler any old day. Sighing, she turned up the sound on the CD.

"You're much stronger than you think you are," intoned the voice. "Honor your Inner Voice. Don't be afraid to roar like a lion when you successfully defy the obstacles that block your progress."

Like…right now?

She was supposed to howl like an animal just because she passed a broken-down trailer? Well...why not? No one could hear her. Her first attempt at a roar sounded suspiciously like a toy poodle with a sore throat. It would have been embarrassing, but after suffering through two hours of "From Wimp to Winner: The Path to Holistic Empowerment," embarrassment was no longer an issue.

"RAGGGGGH!"

This time she scared herself because the brunt of her aria was directed against the well-meaning friend who'd given her the CD for Christmas. Did Nancy really think Jessica was a weak-willed doormat who needed an emergency ego transplant? *Nobody* who'd seen Jessica Stratton in action at Sotheby's auction house last week would brand her as pushover.

She'd held her own. Think of the sheer steely *nerve* it had taken to outbid those hard-as-nails New York dealers. Jessica muted the sound and re-experienced the rush of adrenalin she'd felt when the auctioneer smacked the hammer down. She'd secured a vintage Quaker desk—exactly what a major client needed for his picture-perfect home office—and at a considerable profit for Stratton Gallery.

But had she roared like a lion after she closed the deal?

Of course not.

Max said "Good girl" when she phoned him from New York right after the sale. *Good girl*! And she'd practically rolled on the rug in ecstasy, like a kitty with a catnip toy. Jessica winced at the memory.

Whereas Max Stratton got whatever he wanted without roaring. To her knowledge, he had never raised his voice at all if one discounted a few judicious "Bravos" at Symphony Hall. Why would Max bother to raise his *voice*? All he needed to do was raise an eyebrow and watch the opposition crumple into dust.

Like Jessica had crumpled last night when—once again—Max vetoed the idea of a summer vacation together in the Cape Cod house and announced the Italian plans. That's why she'd rooted ''From Wimp to Winner'' out of its post-Christmas exile in the back pantry this morning. Brushing a stray lock of hair out of her eyes, Jessica turned up the volume and forced herself to pay attention. Maybe there was something in this Self-Empowerment mumbo-jumbo that she could put to use.

The scenery was already weaving its rural spell. Scraggy Cape Cod pine trees had gradually replaced the lusher vegetation that had lined the road when she left Boston a few hours ago. By the time Jessica turned off the Route 6 highway at the Brewster exit, the gray-beige sand had crept over the edges of the blacktop. The air already held a lick of the salt breezes that dyed the golden cedar wall shingles of Cape Cod buildings to the weathered gray of oyster shells after a few years. It made the local houses look like they rose, fully formed, from the chilly Atlantic waters into the morning mists.

"Tap into the Cosmic Energy field and channel your Inner Voice whenever you have doubts…"

Jessica waved to the farmer in the roadside vegetable stand as she drove past Brewster's historic town center, represented by a graceful wooden church and a Victorian-style General Store. She was almost home. Well, not exactly home. That was what last night's argument had been about, wasn't it? Jessica sighed again, and turned off Route 6A into the driveway of the Disputed Territory.

Morning fog, still thick in patches between the pine trunks, blurred the roof of the house, but the slate shingles, white clapboard sides, and black wooden shutters exemplified the simple austerity of classic New England architecture. The beveled fanlight over the front door bore witness to the wealth of the whaling captain who'd commissioned the house in 1781. Single-story cedar additions, attached helter-skelter from the back door in time-honored Cape Cod tradition, attested to the needs of the growing families who'd occupied the house over the next two hundred years.

The outside walls and the interior stairwell had settled off-kilter over the years, but that only added to the house's period charm. In fact, *nothing* detracted from the charm in Jessica's opinion. All the house needed was to be lived in and loved. Jessica sketched in a rose-laden trellis, a calico cat sleeping on the front walk, the aroma of fresh bread wafting through the windows.

Well, fresh bread was a reach. A frozen baguette thawed out in a microwave would be more like it. If you were one half of "the powerhouse couple who run Beacon Hill's most exclusive American Art gallery"— as last week's article in the *Boston Globe* had defined her—there simply wasn't time to spare for retro pastimes like baking bread.

She watched two gray squirrels as they scampered merrily across the front lawn. The squirrels, at least, were full time residents. She eyed them resentfully and switched off the motor. The voice of the holistic empowerment guru trailed off in mid-sentence.

Since this was just a routine visit, a spot-check to assess repairs before the summer season began, she might as well get started on her own. Nancy Webster, the real estate agent who handled the vacation rentals, would be along in a few minutes with a clipboard full of scribbled recommendations and an entire winter's worth of gossip. A few precious moments, in which Jessica could pretend she actually lived in the house, was always a special treat to be savored.

Walking up the flagstone path to the front door, Jessica noted that one of the downstairs shutters was hanging awry, swinging back and forth on its hinges. The winter storms had been especially violent this year but Cape Cod problems like this one were delightfully easy to resolve: a phone call, a hammer, a nail, and a lick of paint could solve almost anything. She'd have to make an appointment with the landscaping company too. Thick, leathery clumps of matted oak leaves blanketed most of the garden, and the lavender-blue hydrangea bushes were in dire need of some professional TLC.

Jessica had the house keys ready before she realized that something was wrong. Really, really wrong. The sleek wood around the brass lock was a bird's nest of paint shards and splintered wood.

She caught her breath. A break-in? And the damn thing was, the break-in could have happened yesterday…or it could have happened months ago. Who would have thought to notify her? Nancy drove by frequently but while she'd have noticed if the place had burned down, she didn't check out the interior on a regular basis. The nearest neighbors would normally be the retirees in the cottage across the street, but their place had been empty since their move to Florida last October. There wasn't a soul in sight, nor a sound to be heard, except for the gentle swish of the loose shutter and the chirping of the robins.

And Jessica's Inner Voice.

Right now, that Inner Voice was screaming like an out of control banshee: "*Run away! Call the police! Forget the police! Call the FBI!*" But as Jessica tentatively ran her fingers over the damaged lock, the heavy oak door swung open with an agonizingly slow screech that sounded as loud as a fire alarm. She flattened herself against the wooden siding, waiting for something horrible to jump out.

Nothing happened. At least not yet.

Cautiously, she stepped over the threshold and peered into the front hall. The interior was dark, but the broken shutter allowed a slender ray of morning sunlight into the living room. It didn't look like anything had been vandalized, and she practically shuddered with relief. The glass bookcases were in place, at any rate, and the pictures were still on the wall.

Panic was beginning to give way to anger and curiosity. Still ready to sprint for safety if necessary, she crept into the hall and looked around for anything that was out of place.

And there it was.

A tomato-red sleeping bag spread out on the antique rag rug in the living room.

And somebody was in it, too. Sprawled out, face down.

Now what was she supposed to do?

Call the police? Nice idea, but she'd forgotten to charge her cell. Unfortunately, the landline was located on the coffee table, just a few feet away from the sleeping bag.

Go outside and wait for back-up assistance? Back-up assistance would be Nancy and honestly, how much help would ninety-pound real estate agent be if things got nasty? Could she brain this guy with her clipboard?

There was always Choice Three.

Namely, charging into the living room like a soon-to-be-expendable extra in an action movie. She could almost hear the imaginary audience screaming, "Don't be so stupid!"

She had to agree. That would be a pretty stupid move, but on the other hand, it was outrageously annoying to be shivering in the doorway while some uninvited guest snoozed happily inside. Frankly, it was bad enough to turn her precious house over to credit-checked tenants who paid dearly for the privilege. Now she had to deal with squatters?

Jessica glared at the intruder, and as her eyes adjusted to the dim light, she distinguished a mass of long, dark hair spilling across a needlepoint cushion that had been appropriated from the loveseat to serve as a bed-pillow.

A woman?

This was too much. She was being turned out of her house by a girl? She deserved to be branded as a wimp if she couldn't handle this by herself. Jessica tapped into the Cosmic Energy Field and got in touch with the desire to sweep an obstacle out of her living room.

However, as she edged up toward the coffee table, she stopped by the fireplace to pick up the wrought iron poker. Just in case. For all she knew, Sleeping Beauty had listened to some Holistic Empowerment tapes of her own.

An ancient pine floorboard creaked under Jessica's foot as she crept across the room for a closer look. She held her breath as the slippery, synthetic fabric of the sleeping bag rustled. Then a surprisingly husky growl rumbled from its down-filled depths.

"Mmmmmph?"

Jessica froze.

"Martine?"

Still asleep, the intruder rolled over, exposing a broad, bronzed, and decidedly masculine torso. A technical book, filled with intricate graphs and mathematical equations, lay open at his side. A cup of tea, in one of Jessica's prized China Export cups, chilled on the table beside a carefully folded pair of jeans and a flannel work shirt.

Whoever this guy was, he had made himself utterly at home.

Now what?

Her Inner Voice had clammed up suddenly, so Jessica was on her own. The floorboard creaked again as soon she shifted her weight. *Nancy, where the hell are you!* Taking a deep breath, Jessica trained her art dealer's eye for detail onto the intruder's physique. Maybe she could pick up some clues about who she was facing.

One thing was sure. She didn't want to grapple with him one-on-one. He looked terribly strong. Lean, yes, but it looked like his muscles had muscles. Framed against the exotic, shoulder-length black hair, the sleeper's face radiated assurance. He looked like someone who could let out a pretty strong roar whenever he felt like it too. The outlaw's straight, aquiline nose was offset by dark, uncompromising eyebrows. Unfortunately, "outlaw" and "uncompromising" were the first words that came to her mind and those, thought Jessica uneasily, were not exactly reassuring under the circumstances. However, the mouth looked generous, with laugh lines suggesting that he knew how to smile. Thirty, maybe thirty-five years old, she guessed.

Handsome? Extremely. Intelligent? Educated? Very likely, given the reading matter. Non-conformist? Probably. With hair like that, it was safe bet that he wasn't an investment banker. And powerful? Absolutely. She could read that even through the oddly vulnerable calm of the sleeper's face.

The point was, he really didn't look like a criminal.

But neither did Ted Bundy, prompted Jessica's suddenly loquacious Inner Voice. Neither did Frederick West. Neither—it was unsafe to say—did Jack the Ripper.

Dropping to her knees, Jessica crawled toward the telephone stealthily, and, when she had it in hand, drew back and pressed "O."

"Operator."

"Can you get me the—"

"I can't hear you, ma'am. Please speak up loud and clear."

For heaven's sake, if she felt safe speaking up loud and clear, she wouldn't need the police. Very cautiously, Jessica turned her back to the intruder, pressed her lips into the mouthpiece, and tried again.

"Can you get me the—"

"HEY!"

A powerful hand grabbed her arm, dropping Jessica to a seated position with a loud thump. The telephone and the poker clattered to the floor.

"WHO THE HELL ARE YOU?" The voice was low but possessed the thunderous clout of authority. "WHAT ARE YOU SNEAKING AROUND HERE FOR?"

"I live here," hissed Jessica, struggling to free her arm.

"Try again," said her captor inflexibly, but not without a trace of humor in his voice as his eyes swept over the furniture draped in dustsheets. "Nobody lives here, and the owner's in Boston."

"I'm the owner!" cried Jessica angrily. "And you better let me go or I'll have you arrested for…"

"Mrs. Stratton?" The iron grip relaxed, and Jessica used the instant to back away. "Are you Mrs. Stratton?" The stranger rubbed his eyes and when he opened them, Jessica was waving the poker menacingly in his face. "What the…?"

Jessica knelt by the phone and picked up the receiver.

"Ma'am? Are you all right?"

"Everything's fine," said Jessica. "I've got the situation under control."

What an understatement! She'd gone from "Wimp" to "Winner" in a two-hour drive! She'd besieged her very own castle, she'd conquered it, and she'd taken a prisoner as well. She hung up the phone and addressed her captive with the proud and well-earned condescension of a victorious general. Frankly, it felt good to be in control for a change.

"I'm sure that you appreciate the fact that I haven't

brought the police into this," she began, "but I have to insist on some explanations."

"Such as?"

The bubble burst. She hadn't expected any backtalk. To her surprise, the stranger lay back on the pillow, placed his arms behind his head, and stared at the ceiling.

"Let's start with the obvious ones," she said icily. "Like who you are and what you're doing here?"

"Would you please put down that ridiculous weapon first?"

Jessica shook her head.

"May I have my pants?"

"NO!"

Evidently unwilling to take "NO" for an answer, he raised himself up on one elbow and coolly reached toward the table for his jeans.

But Jessica was faster.

The tip of the poker slipped into the belt loop and tossed the denims across the room before he could lay his hands on them. A glimpse of thigh as he stretched across the table indicated that he wasn't wearing much else besides the sleeping bag.

Furious but silent, he lay back on the floor and resumed his study of the ceiling.

"Who are you?" she asked again.

"I'll answer that if you ask nicely."

And now he's dictating the protocol! Jessica sighed in exasperation and surrendered the point.

"If you would be so kind."

"Name: Rick Starfire Martell. Address: Across the street. Status: Unarmed. Now that that's settled, would you please put down the poker before you hurt someone?"

"Not yet," replied Jessica testily. "What are you doing in my house?"

"Being a Good Samaritan, that's what!" Eyes flashing, the stranger scrambled to his feet, tucking the sleeping bag around his waist. "I should never have let Nancy talk me into it either, if this is how people in New England express their gratitude."

"Nancy? Nancy Webster?"

"Who else? She came by with my lease last night and noticed that someone had jimmied your door. I offered to pinch-hit as caretaker until the locksmith showed up this morning. End of story."

"If that's true, I'm—"

"*If that's true!*" Rick swore under his breath, and then stared at the ceiling again, as if searching for divine inspiration.

Jessica felt like she could use some celestial guidance herself. If this man's story checked out, she owed him an apology, but in the meantime…

"Look," she said. "The lock's broken, you're a perfect stranger, and Nancy didn't tell me anything about this. What am I supposed to think?"

The lights flickered on, and both Jessica and Rick started.

"Sorry I'm late." Nancy Webster stood in the doorway, blinking as her eyes adjusted to the artificial light. "Jessica, I didn't get a chance to tell you about… Oh, I see you two already met. Hi, Rick. Anyone try to steal anything?"

"Besides my good name and reputation?" Rick sank back into Jessica's Adirondack rocking chair, still cocooned in his red nylon wrap. "Better vouch for me,

Nancy, before this madwoman calls in the SWAT team."

But Nancy's shrewd green eyes had already assessed the situation. Jessica, white-faced, poised to lead the Light Brigade with an iron poker. Rick, bare-chested and wrapped to waist in a sleeping bag. While her friend attributed her remarkable sales skills to an eerie sixth sense, Nancy didn't need ESP to register the tension in this living room.

"Relax, Rick's one of the good guys, Jessica." Nancy pried the poker from her friend's fingers and pushed her gently toward the kitchen. "Let's get the coffee on. And Rick," she added over her shoulder, "how about getting some clothes on? We'll have breakfast ready in five minutes, okay?"

Chapter Two

"Nancy, why didn't you warn me?" moaned Jessica as she sank into the nearest kitchen chair and buried her head in her hands.

"I just hated the idea of you worrying all night for nothing, that's all." Nancy pulled up a chair and patted Jessica's shoulder. "By the time I went through the rental checklist to see if anything was missing—nothing's gone, honey, not even a cookie tin—it was awfully late. The crooks must have been scared off right after they broke the lock. Rick was helping me, and then he offered to guard the door in case they came back…and that's that."

"Well, I just rushed in and accused him of breaking in. I was so scared…and angry! Nancy, I don't know when I've been so angry. And then he wouldn't tell me who he was until I said 'please'…"

"It's the magic word, isn't it?" Nancy took three mugs from the shelf over the sink. "I had every intention of being here before you got here so I could make formal introductions but getting a fifteen-year-old with a bad hair day off to school is like a national security crisis on steroids." Nancy chuckled. "Anyway, it was almost worth it to see you holding off the enemy with that toasting fork or whatever. My goodness, Jessica, I never thought you had it in you. You're always so quiet and demure, never speaking up to that stuck-up husband of yours…"

Jessica raised her eyebrows.

"Sorry, kid. I'm sure Max isn't stuck-up, he just seems that way to me, but what do I know? Anyway, you looked like a superhero fending off the Martian Army of Evil. I wish I'd thought to take a picture."

"Well, this place is my sacred home planet," said Jessica, looking around the kitchen as if reassuring herself it was all in one piece. "Finding some perfect stranger in one's house is a rough way to start the morning."

"Exactly what I said to Melanie when she walked into the kitchen with a scarf and giant sunglasses." Nancy handed Jessica the coffee pot. "Get the water on, and I'll rinse out some mugs. Yuck, the dust that accumulates in a place over six months! By the way, Rick is not some 'perfect stranger' as you put it. I rented him that cottage across the street so he's your neighbor now. Like most of these out-of-towners, he was holding out for a place closer to the water, but I got him a terrific price and I think he'll be happy there."

"Happier when I leave, I'm sure."

"Phooey. First impressions should be against the law. Rick ought to be dressed by now. Go ask him if he wants milk and sugar in his coffee. I brought some from home."

The slam of the front door echoed through the house.

"I expect that means 'no'," said Jessica.

She walked into the living room, raised the window, and opened the shutters. Cool morning light flooded the empty room. No trace of the sleeping bag. The pillow was back in place on the loveseat although the poker lay on the floor like a discarded sword. Nancy joined her at the window just as a dark-green jeep hurtled out of the driveway across the street.

"Well, he'll get over it. I'll have a word with him if you don't run into him sooner." Nancy shrugged. "I guess it's just the two of us for breakfast, but we've got a few hours before the locksmith gets here with a hard sell on alarm systems. I swear these guys break into houses themselves to stir up business. Why don't you air out the bedrooms while I set the table?"

The eighteenth-century staircase was so narrow that Jessica wondered how her tenants ever got their giant suitcases into the two small bedrooms. Originally there had been three bedrooms, but the former owner had converted one into a luxurious bathroom. Ezra Wilder, the Puritan whaling captain who built the house, would have considered the double-wide shower positively indecent. On the other hand, he might have liked the idea of washing his sheep and his horse inside for a change if he could get the livestock up the stairs. Jessica made a mental note about a slight discoloration around the bathroom sink and moved on.

The pink bedroom was her favorite: pale rose woodblock wallpaper, handwoven rugs, and a glossy, walnut-stained hardwood floor. The fourposter bed, topped with an ivory netted canopy, was her treasure. No wonder her vacationing tenants raved about it. They probably spent gloriously romantic weekends beneath that canopy. How long had it been since *she* had a romantic weekend?

Was that long winter weekend in New York supposed to count? She'd been stuck all day in the auction house, Max was off somewhere in Long Island giving estimates on an estate sale, and they'd spent both evenings at dinner with demanding clients. The Four Seasons was a lovely hotel, but they hadn't done anything there except fall asleep, utterly exhausted, as soon as they got back to the room.

Jessica stopped short in front of the bedroom mirror and swept her shoulder length, ash-blonde hair— laboriously blow-dried and styled in the sophisticated society pageboy that was almost *de rigueur* in Boston's WASPy aristocracy—into a loose bun.

The dusty mirror, streaked with cobwebs, gave a fuzzy, sepia cast to her reflection. For a moment, Jessica closed her eyes and imagined living in Colonial Massachusetts. No phone. No internet. No high-pressure auction sales. No store-bought cinnamon potpourri to make the house smell like a home. Just the simple, honest aroma of home cooking. She wrinkled her nose. Was it her imagination? Or did she really sniff fresh pastry baking?

"Jessica!" Nancy's plaintive voice shattered the reverie. "I haven't had breakfast yet, and Rick left some super-looking date bread which I'm re-heating. It's gonna be charcoal-flavored if you don't get down here fast."

Jessica rubbed a clean center in the mirror and gave her reflection a last, searching look. Nancy was pulling a tin cake pan from the oven when she reached the kitchen.

"Smells great, doesn't it? Rick said he'd bring something for breakfast. Wonder if he made it himself?" Nancy giggled. "If he did, you can accuse the poor guy of baking and entering." She cut two slices and laid them on the plates. "Here's an extra-large one for you, Jessica. You look like you need it. Has Max been working you too hard?"

Jessica smiled as Nancy warmed up for a full-fledged maternal onslaught. At thirty-two, Jessica was only twelve years her junior, but Nancy had been forced to assume an authoritative voice with her own daughter after her husband died of a stroke two years ago. The excess mothering tended to spill over into her relations with Jessica and her clients.

Jessica, on the other hand, had taken on the role of a glamorous older sister for Nancy's daughter, Melanie. Melanie's spring term adventures at Nauset High School took them through the first cup of coffee. Nancy's scathing rundown of the current real estate market took them through the next.

"Honestly, it's the same old, same old. Too many people expect something for nothing these days," she concluded, pausing to lick a breadcrumb from her finger. "On the plus side, I've got a Wall Street tycoon who'll break the bank if I find him the right waterfront property. How's business in Boston?"

"No millionaire clients at the moment," Jessica confessed. "Though I've had an interesting proposition."

Nancy looked up. "Do tell. Is he cute? Rich? Single?"

"She's my old college roommate," continued Jessica without missing a beat. "She's producing a cable show about home decoration and wants me to discuss American Folk Art."

Nancy whistled appreciatively. "A star is born."

"Not necessarily. I haven't said yes."

"But you have to! You've been collecting that stuff

for years, and you never do anything with it. Opportunities like this don't come around every day."

"But Nancy…"

"But what?"

"She wants to film it at 'my place' and I don't even have a showroom. My collection isn't even on display at our house. I'll look like a nut case if I'm dragging a television crew up to the attic."

Years ago, Max had decreed that Jessica's eclectic collection of quilts, samplers, store signs, cast iron doorstops and weathervanes would detract from the formal antiques and artwork that he sold at the Stratton Gallery. In return for Jessica's reluctant agreement, he'd promised that they'd eventually look for a shopfront in Boston of her own.

So far, something else always took priority, like new lighting or extra advertising for the Stratton Gallery. Nancy had suspected for a long time that Max Stratton had no intention of letting his wife (and full-time, unpaid office manager and sales assistant) stake out her own place in the sun. "A blue-blooded bluefish" was Nancy's take on Max Stratton. She remembered how encouraging Ted had been when she studied for the real estate exam and how proud he'd been when she made her first sale. She began to feel tears burning and tried to concentrate on what Jessica was saying.

"…a darling little boutique just around the corner, but Max thinks the recession is bound to continue so we…"

"We?" Now Nancy raised her eyebrows.

"We thought it would be better to wait until next year."

Nancy looked at her friend thoughtfully. There had

to be a way around this.

"Say, Jessica, how are you and Max doing for money these days? The gallery's doing fine, right?"

"Better than ever…"

"In that case, you really don't need the rental income on this place this summer?"

"I suppose not. What's your point?"

"Set up your own shop here! It's right on Route 6A and it's already zoned for business. Cape Cod will be crawling with antique buffs and rich tourists after Memorial Day."

"Nancy, it just might work," said Jessica after a long pause. "Of course, Max will say it's madness."

"Genius and madness go together. I'm the perfect example of that adage. I've never talked myself out of a commission before."

"A commission that you're just as happy to lose, I suspect," said Jessica with a sly grin. "I'm probably the fussiest landlord on your roster."

"You bet! Don't let them scuff the woodwork. Don't let them spill chowder on the Chippendale. Don't let—"

"I'll make it up to you with shop discounts and easy credit, wait and see." Then Jessica's smile faded. "But I'd need permits, wouldn't I?"

"I don't think there will be too much paperwork. The folks over at Town Hall are always in favor of scenic, non-polluting business. I've got some friends over there. Why don't I check into that for you?"

"Then…"

"Then it's all settled." Nancy beamed at her friend triumphantly. "You won't wriggle out of this one. You'll be a rich and famous cable TV star with a shop of your own whether you like it or not."

"Nancy, you make everything sound a little too easy."

"Heck, other people's problems are easy. Now it's your turn to solve mine. Melanie wants to get her nose pierced. What on earth…?"

Chapter Three

The sun was low, but Jessica's spirits were high as her trusty sedan skimmed across the Sagamore Bridge and headed up Route 3 to Boston. *Wilder House Antiques.* That was the name she wanted. Nancy had pushed for "Jessica's Junkyard" all through lunch...but in vain. Max would break out in hives if she confronted him with a name like that. He had a Boston Brahmin's allergy to "cute."

"Cute" was an easy pitfall to avoid, but Max was likely to zero in on some other weak link in her plan. But, to her growing delight, the more she thought about it, the more she was convinced that Wilder House Antiques would just *have* to open. After all, as Nancy had remarked many times before, Jessica was an equal partner in every aspect of Stratton Gallery except decision-making.

"If Max gives you any grief, tell him I'll park my rattletrap station wagon in front of his snooty old gallery until he gives in," was Nancy's parting shot as they said goodbye.

A typical Nancy solution. The only trouble with Nancy, thought Jessica, was her complete and utter lack of romance. "Cash on the barrel." "Get it in black and white." Her favorite motto—which she'd engraved on her ID bracelet—was a quote from hockey star Wayne Gretzky: "You miss 100 percent of the shots you don't take." That summed up Nancy's philosophy.

The only time the women had ever argued was over an illustrated edition of *Grimm's Fairy Tales* that Jessica had given Melanie for her tenth birthday. "No way will I let my kid grow up thinking that Prince Charming with a Gold Card is gonna make all her dreams come true," Nancy had stormed. Jessica took the book back and exchanged it for *Nancy Drew and the Sign of the Twisted Candles*, and her friend approved heartily. "Aside from the fact that the girl has a super-cool first name, she's one hell of a lot more proactive than Snow White. That babe almost snoozed her life away in a coffin while she was waiting for some clown to kiss her."

All things considered, it was only natural that Nancy couldn't understand Jessica's marriage which was, after all, a modern-day Cinderella story.

At twenty-one, Jessica had a freshly minted diploma in American History from Boston College, a hefty student loan to pay back, and barely enough cash to pay for a cheeseburger. If there were any jobs around, they weren't coming her way. Of course, she could always go home. Back to Lowell Mills, a permanently depressed New England factory town where the industry's smoke was thick enough to dim the fall foliage. After the bright lights of Boston, going back to Lowell Mills would feel like a prison sentence.

"Stratton Gallery, American Antiques" caught her eye when she'd got to the point where she was applying to any business that had the word "American" in it. As soon as she stepped in the Back Bay doorway, she knew she was out of her league. The soft lights, thick carpets, and burnished wood were intimidating enough, and her navy suit, a designer copy bought on markdown, suddenly looked as if it had "Filene's Basement" embroidered on the lapel. She was about to turn tail when...

"May I help you?"

The most elegant man she'd ever seen rose from behind a mahogany desk. Tall, slim, dark hair...plus a pencil moustache that gave him the look of a 1940s matinee idol.

"May I help you?" he repeated.

"I was looking for a job."

"Ah, miss...?"

"Paquette. Jessica Paquette."

"French?"

"French Canadian."

"Well, Miss Paquette, do you know anything about antiques?"

Jessica thought of everything her roommate had coached her to say in such situations. ("If you can't bluff about your experience, tell them a big fat lie," advised her roommate. That policy had already snagged Chris an internship at a local TV station.)

But these flinty gray eyes looked alarmingly bluff-proof.

"Nothing at all, but I'd like to learn."

"Very well, Miss Paquette. Come in at 10 o'clock tomorrow and prepare to learn." He sat down and picked up the phone.

Jessica was stunned.

He looked up. "You wanted a job, didn't you? You have one. Now leave."

For the next six months, Jessica answered the phone, polished silver, read everything she could about the antiques market, and worshiped Max Stratton. Though tantalizingly aloof, he was a born teacher, and Jessica proved to be a quick learner with a natural eye for fine lines and craftsmanship.

By haunting the fancier second-hand shops, she assembled a wardrobe wouldn't embarrass her in front of the Back Bay debutantes who popped into the boutique ostensibly in search of landscape paintings by John Frederick Kensett or Queen Anne silver services. However, neither these pampered heiresses nor their mothers ever stuck around for more than a few minutes if Max was out of the office.

Which made it all the more surprising when Max asked her to accompany him to a charity gala organized by his mother, the unofficial empress of Boston society. For Jessica, the meal passed in a blur of crystal wineglasses, bizarre vegetables, and bewildering silverware options. Dierdre Kingsley Stratton dominated most of the conversation with tales of her recent trip to Cap d'Antibes, which Jessica belatedly realized was a resort in France.

Max was so silent as he drove her home that Jessica figured she'd eaten the cake with the fish fork and was on her way to being fired.

She braced herself for the worst.

Instead, he asked her to marry him.

Mrs. Stratton retired to Palm Beach shortly after the wedding and, in fact, it was Jessica's ancient Aunt Kate who voiced the only objection to the match. Like Nancy, she just didn't believe in fairy tales. "And Max and I have been together for ten years, so for once Aunt Kate got it wrong," thought Jessica smugly as she left the highway and edged into Boston's rush hour traffic.

Ten years. The anniversary was in three weeks and for once, Jessica was glad that Max didn't believe in big parties and lavish gifts for sentimental occasions. However, he was very fond of anything that sounded like an investment...as long as the investment was "safe" and would add luster to the Stratton Gallery. That was the way she'd present Wilder House. As an investment that would expand the Stratton "brand" and pay for itself.

She glanced at the dashboard clock. Max had been at a conference in North Carolina for the past few days and his plane was due at Logan at 7 p.m. She'd have plenty of time to shower, chill his favorite wine, order a fancy dinner from the gourmet shop, and be ready to surprise him with the new idea when he got home.

She parked behind the townhouse and strode up to the back door. There was no reason she couldn't make a persuasive case for Wilder House. Her attention flitted to the window boxes that she usually planted with fresh basil every spring. *Maybe not this year,* she thought as she fished through her purse for her keys, *since Max will never remember to water them if I'm on the Cape.*

Then she caught her breath. The door was ajar.

No, no, no, NO!

Not *another* break-in? *Two* break-ins in one day?

This was getting old...

Chapter Four

Before she could work up a full-scale panic attack, Max Stratton pushed the door wide open.

"Darling, where have you been all day?"

"What?"

"Anyone would think you weren't pleased to see me." Max Stratton leaned against the door, as graceful, languid, and meticulously stylish as usual.

Jessica kissed his cheek lightly and shrugged out of her sweater. She detected a hint of alcohol on his breath, and that was odd. Scotch in the afternoon was not his usual style. "Of course, I'm glad to see you. What are you doing back so early?"

"The damned flight left at 5:30 a.m., not 5:30 p.m. as printed on the itinerary. By the time I figured that out last night, it was too late to call."

"Max, I'm thrilled that you're back, and I've got so much to tell you. A big surprise." The words were rushing out now. So much for staying cool and collected. "I went down to the Cape today, and you'll never guess what happened. What I thought of…actually…what Nancy thought of. It's…"

Max pointed to the living room. "Could it wait until dinner? I've got a surprise of my own in there."

"Max! You finally got that Hepplewhite chair?" cried Jessica in delight.

"No, it's something bigger than an armchair," said

Max, following her into the parlor.

"I should hope so!" came a booming voice from across the room. Edward Fairweather Winthrop III stood, or rather lounged, against the fireplace. Eddie Winthrop, ex-associate of Stratton Galleries. Max's prep school roommate.

When was the last time he'd showed up? It must have been about three years ago. Same strawberry blond hair and turquoise eyes, though his once-muscular All-American frame was showing the first signs of bloat. But not *ordinary* middle-age spread since Eddie would never develop anything as mundane as a beer belly. This would have to be a very expensive brandy belly. Nevertheless, he was still handsome enough to turn heads. Why he'd never married, with his looks and lineage, was a puzzle.

"Back from your afternoon tryst with the sexy firefighter?" he inquired.

"*Mais oui*, Eddie, it was very *romantique*." Jessica smiled at him sweetly. She wouldn't let him get her goat as easily as he usually did. "What brings you to town?"

"He's coming home to Boston! Isn't that wonderful, Jessica? He's been larking around Europe for so long that I was starting to suspect that his business was sneaking contraband through customs."

"Max's imagination will do him in some day." Eddie scowled and poured himself a liberal shot of single malt whisky from a crystal decanter on the sideboard. "I finally realized that there's no place like home. Missed my roots and all that. Max, don't you remember that party when we got up on the table and swore that we'd live and die Bostonian?"

"God, you were so drunk that night!"

"Me? Whose idea was it to throw the lobster at Tracy?"

"Lobsters? Who threw any lobsters?"

Now they were laughing hysterically and barely noticed when Jessica excused herself. Maybe that was the reason she resented Eddie so much. It wasn't simply that he never missed a chance to talk about country clubs, debutante cotillions, polo matches and all sorts of places and people that left Jessica out. What was worse was the way that Max relaxed with Eddie, like he never relaxed with her.

Well, there goes my chance to present Wilder House Antiques tonight. Jessica retreated to the kitchen and reached for a big bag of tagliatelle on the pantry shelf. She'd serve her home-made pesto sauce with it, and some slices of smoked salmon on the side. Pesto was the only "home-made" recipe in her limited kitchen repertoire…and that was because pesto didn't have to be cooked. Any recipe that required serious oven time generally fizzled under Jessica's watch, but pesto was just a matter of mashing up basil leaves with a handful of pine nuts, some parmesan cheese, garlic, and olive oil. It was love at first bite when she tasted the emerald-green sauce on her Italian honeymoon. Jessica always kept at least one jar of it on hand for emergencies ever since.

After a long soak in the tub, the evening's prospects looked a little brighter. Maybe Eddie's presence would be a blessing in disguise. Eddie had a gambler's appetite for risk and far more enthusiasm for entrepreneurial schemes than Max. And for once, Eddie's innate nastiness might work in Jessica's favor.

"He'd be just mean enough to want me fall on my face if Wilder House fails," thought Jessica with the fervor of a newly converted ex-wimp. "Not that I intend to let it fail."

After some reflection, she decided on a beige cashmere sweater and a pair of slim, chocolate-brown suede pants that skimmed, rather than hugged, her hips. Jessica was often tempted to jazz up her Max-approved, ultra-WASP wardrobe with an offbeat African necklace or a colorful scarf, but not tonight. Tonight she'd try to look as much like the Perfect Preppie as she could. She slipped into a pair of trim brown loafers. Since her make-up skills were as minimal as her cooking credentials, she contented herself with a dab of rose lipstick and the lightest possible hint of moss-green shadow on her eyelids.

Back in the kitchen, she put the water on to boil and sliced some lemon wedges for the salmon. Whew! Slicing lemons, opening a jar of pesto, removing the sliced salmon from its delicatessen wrap, and boiling water for the pasta...no one could accuse her of slacking off on the culinary front tonight! Tomorrow, things would be back to normal. Take-out food if she was dining with Max, or crackers and cheese if she was alone. She poured herself a glass of mineral water and headed for the living room.

"Dinner at eight, boys," she said as she switched on the stained-glass Tiffany lamp which brought a soft glow to the formal room. Max was sitting with exaggerated stiffness in one of the Windsor chairs near the fireplace, and Eddie was sprawled across the loveseat. The silver ice bucket was by his feet, its rim leaving a watermark on the polished hardwood floor, but for once, Max hardly seemed to notice. Jessica crossed the room to pick it up.

"Dinner at eight? That's marvelous," said Max.

"And what's for dinner tonight?" asked Eddie.

"Tagliatelle and pesto, salmon, and salad," said Jessica.

"Presto, it's pesto," giggled Eddie. "Max, that sounds like the perfect occasion for some of excellent Château Clos d'Estournal that you save for your best and oldest friends."

"I think you've had quite enough of my Scotch tonight," said Max sharply. "California Chablis will be fine."

"Your miserly cruelty offends me, Max. Jessica, dear, what's all this about a surprise? It can't be the pesto. Jessica made it the last time I was here. Maybe you eat too much pesto, Max? Maybe that's why you look so green around the gills?"

"Jessica's surprise has something to do with Cape Cod, Eddie."

"Jessica, have you found yourself a red-hot lover down there? Someone who makes you forget about poor, green Max?"

"Oh, cut it out, Eddie," said Max, smiling in spite of himself. "Jessica, you better tell us about it before Eddie gets himself into trouble."

"Max, I don't want to rent the Brewster house this year." Jessica took a deep breath. "I want to set up a shop for my collection of folk art."

"How about that?" said Eddie a moment later, breaking the silence as he jiggled the ice cubes in his empty glass.

Max's cool, clear voice chimed in with a soothing,

almost paternal tone. "Do you think that this is the right time to start a project like this? The antiques market on the Cape is already saturated."

"Not my specialty. I can make it work."

"Give the little lady a chance, Max. She might start poisoning your pesto if you don't."

"This is none of your business, Eddie," said Max. "Jessica, you're needed at Stratton Gallery. Period."

"Not necessarily," said Eddie slowly. "I'm back in Boston now. There's no reason why I can't lend a hand at the gallery."

Jessica looked up in surprise. Eddie was behaving like an ally? This was far more than she'd hoped for. "Max, I really think it's now or never. I've paid my dues for years."

"Old man, it'll be like old times with both of us together," added Eddie.

"Jessica, are you *sure* this is what you want?" asked Max.

"Absolutely, Max. I've dreamed about this for years."

"I appear to be out-voted," said Max. "I suppose this evening calls for a bottle of Champagne."

"Attaboy," said Eddie, rubbing his hands together. "Bring on the pesto!"

Chapter Five

When anyone asked Jessica how she spent the next few weeks, she'd answer "like a truck driver." She made the six-hour round-trip between Boston and Brewster nearly every day, her car loaded with fragile objects swaddled in sheets, bubble-wrap, and blankets.

Nancy was right when she predicted smooth sailing on the administrative front. Wilder House needed no construction permits, and the back yard had space for six or seven cars. The Historical Society approved Jessica's sign (discreet bayberry blue-on-white) which she promptly ordered from Tony da Silva, a local woodworker.

The expressway traffic moved slowly today, and Jessica stifled a yawn as she crossed the Sagamore Bridge. This morning she'd woken early and rented a minivan to transport the last cumbersome objects: crates of dishes, heavy boxes of reference books, two display cases, a painted rocking chair, a wooden ship's figurehead, and a six-foot-tall cigar store Indian.

"Lady Hiawatha" was Jessica's pet name for the late nineteenth-century statue that Aunt Kate had given Jessica as a wedding present. Garbed in a fanciful toga of vaguely Incan inspiration and coiffed with a cascade of imperial feathers, most of which were broken, the colossus was mounted on an elaborate wooden pedestal with four brass wheels.

Max banished the statue to the attic shortly after the honeymoon. The statue got her revenge when descending three flights of stairs this morning, poking Max in the ribs with her spiked head-dress at least five times.

"Pure unadulterated kitsch and heavy as lead," groaned Max, straining to get a grip on the figure's waist while avoiding the pointed arrows in her quiver. "It's politically incorrect as well. Linking Native Americans with lung cancer."

"She's beautiful though." The statue's eyes were as sad and wise as a Byzantine Madonna's gaze; her bearing as regal as an empress; her gentle smile as sweet and mysterious as Mona Lisa's. "I don't think this statue was mass-produced in a factory. The artist must have been in love with the woman who posed for this."

"Artists have always been swine," snorted Max. "His model was probably a local call girl."

"Sometimes there had to be mutual love and respect between them."

"Sometimes a cigar ad is just a cigar ad," Max wheezed as he caught his breath on the sidewalk. "Thank goodness she's got her own wheels. We can roll her to the van from here."

"Are you sure you won't drive down with me?" asked Jessica after they'd wedged the blanket-wrapped statue between two bookcases. "You haven't seen the way the place has been fixed up."

"I've seen the invoices, thank you very much. New boiler, new window sashes, new security system. One of us has to stay home and make the money to pay for this nonsense."

"When will you admit that my shop might make money?"

Max gave Lady H's booty a disrespectful shove and closed the van doors. "When I see people lining up to buy firewood like this."

Ouch. Jessica hadn't dared tell him that she wasn't planning to stick a price tag on the statue. Weird as it was and scarred with burn marks, it was her only family heirloom. She had no intention of parting with it.

With a sign of relief, Jessica exited the bumper-to-bumper Mid Cape highway and followed the familiar road signs to Brewster. Despite the heavy traffic, she'd made good time. Nancy wouldn't be over with lunch for at least two hours. Jessica stopped off at the General Store to purchase the owner's prize-winning oatmeal cookies—which would be her only "home-baked" contribution to the picnic—and made a quick detour to the garden shop for a flat of basil seedlings.

Once at the house, she raced up the stairs to the master bedroom. She'd already brought down a big box of her college clothes that had been stored in the Boston attic: all the colorful, non-designer stuff she'd worn before Max started supervising her wardrobe. It felt great to slide into her high school jeans, even if they were a little tighter than they were when she'd snipped off the discount chain's tag back in Lowell Mills fifteen years ago.

The denim was just about worn through, and so were the elbows of her favorite Boston College sweatshirt. She carefully folded her beige designer khakis and put them on same hanger as the stylish navy blazer Max gave her for her last birthday. She stretched happily, did a few gentle squats, and was startled by the sound of ripping denim as her knees broke through to freedom. She surveyed the damage in the Chippendale mirror. Her "look" was now totally tenth grade. A pair of paint-stained sneakers completed the ensemble.

An hour later, twenty-four emerald-green sprouts of future spaghetti sauce had been transplanted in two rows along the south side of the house. Jessica didn't notice the scuffed pair of cowboy boots that had crept up noiselessly beside her until she reached around for the watering can. Darn, it was that self-righteous neighbor she'd found camping on her living room floor. Looking up at him from ground level, he seemed to be about eight feet tall. The long raven hair, which had fallen over his shoulders the first time they met, was pulled back in a neat ponytail.

As she scrambled to her feet, a strong arm reached out and drew her up. "Remember me?" he asked.

Oh, rats! What was the guy's name? *Dick? Nick?* If there was one aspect of social etiquette in which Jessica had zero experience, it was apologizing to people whose name she'd forgotten after threatening to crack their heads open with a poker. "Believe me, I am so sorry about…"

"Why don't we skip all that and start over again?" He smiled and held out his hand. "Hi, I'm your new neighbor, Rick Martell."

"Hello, Rick. I'm *your* new neighbor, Jessica Stratton." She pulled off her garden gloves to shake his outstretched hand, grimacing in annoyance as the fabric on the left glove caught on something. The "something" was, as usual, her jumbo-sized diamond engagement ring. For someone like Max, who always preferred understated tokens of wealth and privilege, the flashy ring was an anomaly. Even for Jessica, who grew up a little too close to the poverty line for comfort, the gaudy ring was a bit embarrassing, more suited to a rock star's fiancée than a respectable Boston matron.

Perhaps Rick thought the same thing, given the slight cloud that came over his expression as he took her hand. Thankfully, all he said was, "The pleasure is mine. And now that the introductions are out of the way, shall we get down to work?"

"But there's no more work," said Jessica. "The gardening's finished for the day."

"I meant unloading the van."

"That's awfully kind of you." *Just how obligated did she want to be to this guy?* "You don't have to do that."

"My motives aren't purely altruistic. Nancy promised me lobster salad rolls and all the potato salad I can eat if we get all this stuff into the house before she gets here."

So this was Nancy's idea? Well, Jessica had to admit it was a smart move. All five-foot-three-inches of Nancy Webster wasn't going to be a whole lot of help when it came to shifting everything in the van, including a heavyweight mahogany statue. "Well, you're about to earn every shred of seafood she promised. You won't believe how much stuff I crammed into this truck."

"Not too bad so far," said Rick after the third crate of dishes had been relocated to the kitchen. "You planning a lot of dinner parties?"

"No, it's all for sale. I'll arrange some of the dinner plates on the bookshelves and stock the rest...I don't know...in the garage. Now, we're into the heavy stuff."

They stared into the van, and a remarkably perky female face stared back at them out of her bubble-wrap swaddling. With a double rope of painted green beads, a low-cut red bodice, and a dramatic up-sweep hairdo, she hardly looked a day over 250 years.

"Is this the heavy lifting you were talking about?" said Rick, picking her up. "This little lady barely weighs a thing."

"By the nineteenth century, shipbuilders figured out that full-body figureheads got in the way of steering, and they switched to smaller formats like this and used lighter woods."

"So basically she was a hood ornament for a boat?"

"She was probably patterned after the wife or daughter of the ship's owner. The idea was to have an image with eyes to help the ship 'see' where it was going. The Vikings used monsters on theirs, the Romans used boars, and the Phoenicians favored birds."

"So where do you want me to put Miss GPS?" Rick hesitated on the threshold of the cottage. "It's getting kind of crowded in there."

"Maybe on top of the loveseat?"

"Gotcha."

The rocking chair, weathervanes, and reference books were next. Rick's flannel work shirt was soon dark with sweat. "What would I have done without him?" thought Jessica as she shoved two bulging cartons of paperwork and auction catalogs under the dining room table to get them out of the way.

"You got a dead body in here?" shouted Rick from the van. Jessica hurried outside. Rick wiped his brow and pointed to a clenched mahogany fist that had poked out of its blankets.

"I'll show you." Jessica climbed into the van and started undoing the strings that held the statue's protective padding in place.

When, after a considerable struggle, they finally got the statue upright on the front walk, Rick scratched his head. "I take it that this is one of those overweight figureheads that got phased out?"

"No, this is a nineteenth-century landlubber. Back in the days when few people knew how to read, storeowners used pictorial signs to advertise their wares. I've got a big wooden straight razor that hung outside a barber's shop somewhere. And a thirty-inch pair of molded scissors that belonged to a tailor."

"What's this babe trying to sell?"

"Cigars. Statues like this stood outside tobacco stores in the nineteenth century. She's supposed to be an exotic Indian princess, but I think of her as family."

"You're Indian, too?" Rick looked at her with surprise. "What tribe?"

"Not." Oh rats, Max had been right about the politically incorrect thing. "And you?"

"One-eighth Cherokee." Rick wrinkled his forehead. "Are you saying that American Indians were used as mascots for tobacco? That this kind of statue was widespread?"

"Yes." Jessica didn't know how to sugarcoat this. "They were called Virginians."

"She's supposed to be from Virginia?" Rick snorted. "She looks more like a demented Aztec who got lost in a toga movie. She's got Iroquois-style fringed leggings, a Sioux war-bonnet, and high-heeled boots that she must have borrowed from a French can-

can dancer. There's nothing authentically Native American about her." He tossed the blanket over the statue's outstretched arm.

"I guess it was the general idea…"

"Indians are more than general ideas." Rick rolled up his sleeves. "Some of us are still flesh and blood."

Almost as if Lady Hiawatha was trying to make the situation more awkward than it already was, the statue—which rolled so blithely down a paved city sidewalk this morning—kept digging her wheels into the sandy soil between the driveway and the front door.

"There's actually a market for stuff like this?" asked Rick as the two of them finally tipped her bulk through the front door. It was fortunate that most of the statue's feathered headdress had broken off since there was barely three inches of clearance in the living room. "Who'd want one of these monstrosities around?"

"They're rather collectible these days," said Jessica. Was she really having the very *same* conversation she'd had with Max this morning? "If they're signed by a famous workshop, they can sell for more than $10,000 at auction."

"No kidding?" Rick whistled. "You could do a lot of good with ten grand."

"What do you mean?"

"The cash for this dumb ethnic stereotype could be invested on a reservation where it's needed."

"But I wasn't planning on selling her."

"Oh." Rick looked down at his boots. "You actually *like* that thing?"

"It's kind of an heirloom."

"Ah. A piece of history." Rick plucked the blanket off the statue's arm, folded it, and handed it to Jessica.

"You screened this for smallpox, I hope."

"Rick…"

"That takes care of everything in the van." He turned on his heels.

"Aren't you staying for lunch? Nancy should be here any minute."

"Previous engagement. See you round."

Chapter Six

Damn, muttered Rick to himself as he walked over to his house. Why'd I go all Tribal Council on that poor woman? I'm an Ivy League engineer who grew up in an air-conditioned Houston penthouse where reservations were something you made at French restaurants. I'm just as authentically Indian as that monster paperweight of hers. And there I was, holding forth on Iroquois leggings and Sioux headdresses. The woman probably thinks I'm the editor of *Navajo Vogue*. Of course, I was *right*. But I was *only* right because I proofread my sister's doctoral thesis last month. *Native American Clothing Interpreted by Hollywood—1920 to Present.*

Rick groaned with pleasure as he stepped into the shower. Moving that stuff from the van had been hot, dirty work. He shook his head, and a cascade of water splashed against the shower curtain. When was he going to get used to all this hair? Never mind, he'd promised Lydia that he'd let it grow out for her wedding. He half-wished his sister believed in shorter engagements.

Lydia was the one who'd gone all heritage on the family a few years ago. His parents' parents had been part of the lost Cherokee generation that had been separated from their traditions and carted off to boarding schools to be "assimilated." And his parents were…totally assimilated. But Lydia had gone off to the hinterlands to research her thesis, fallen in love with a starry-eyed activist in the middle of Nowheresville, Oklahoma, and discovered her roots.

And now that Lydia discovered her roots, she wasn't letting *anyone* forget about them.

Rick braided his wet hair quickly and fastened it with a leather tie.

He was hungry too. Why on earth did that woman get under his skin so much? This was the second time he'd stomped off her property. Well, it had a whole lot to do with that chunk of jewelry on her left hand, didn't it? He didn't need anything to do with married women. Never again.

Had he said anything to her that would make them both cringe if they ran into each other in the minimart?

Oh, yeah. *Smallpox*. Well, that was a low blow, considering that she personally hadn't poisoned any of his ancestors. All the fashion stuff was okay. But he'd added something about French can-can boots, hadn't he? Boots which had absolutely *nothing* to do with his sister's thesis. No, those kinky, lace-up boots were part of Martine's Halloween costume last year.

She hadn't taken those boots off either. Not even when they went to bed.

Just thinking about the sex that ensued made him feel like he needed another shower. But then he'd have to dry all that damn hair again. How did women stand all this stuff hanging around their shoulders? He'd read about hermits who refused to cut their hair until they'd atoned for their sins.

Well, Rick Starfire Martell had a *helluva* lot to atone for.

He grabbed his car keys and headed for his jeep.

He hoped he had enough tracking skill to locate a decent cheeseburger in this town.

Chapter Seven

Damn, thought Jessica for the umpteenth time in fifteen minutes. *I let that man get away without even thanking him for all the hard work he'd done.*

She was still dithering about whether to cross the road and apologize.

But apologize for what?

Stealing his ancestral lands?

Of course, in what Anglo-American history books called the French-and-Indian War, her French-Canadian ancestors had fought *with* the Indians. On the other hand, she had that statue. Which was pretty offensive when you thought about it. Dressing a mannequin in Alpine *lederhosen,* a tartan kilt, and a French beret and labeling the result "Generalized European" would offend a lot of people too.

It's just that she'd always loved the statue. But did that count for anything?

Nancy's station wagon swept into the driveway just as Rick's jeep headed out to the main road.

"Was that Rick?" asked Nancy as she unloaded a blue Styrofoam ice chest from the back seat. "Is he going out for a six-pack or soda or something? I brought everything we need. Didn't you tell him?"

"I'm afraid we told each other too much."

"No, no, NO!" Nancy groaned. "The last time I came here, I thought you were going to stab the poor

46

guy to death. What's happened now?"

"That," said Jessica, nodding to Lady Hiawatha as she carried the carton into the kitchen.

"Good grief!" exclaimed Nancy. "Bring me a beer and tell me whatever the hell 'that' is supposed to be."

Jessica popped two cans of beer and brought them to the living room.

"She's a nineteenth-century tobacco ad."

"Y'know, she looks weirdly Indian. Did I mention that Rick's part…"

"Cherokee? Yep, it came up in the conversation."

"Did he…"

"He finds the statue highly offensive."

"Hummph." Nancy took a long pull on the beer. "Destiny does not want the two of you to get cozy. But tell me, why would anyone want something as weird and whacko as all that in their living room?"

"Are you the *third* person who's asking me that today?"

"Must be a good question."

"It's an heirloom."

"Anything that wasn't glued together in China last night is somebody's heirloom," said Nancy. "How did this particular thingamajig wind up as your heirloom?"

"Ever hear of Briarcrest?"

"Nope."

"It was one of those big turreted mansions in the Berkshire Mountains. My great-grandfather was the caretaker. And when the place burned to the ground on July fourth, 1885…"

"Oh rats!" interrupted Nancy. "The place burned down? You know I *hate* real estate stories with sad endings."

"It was even sadder for the owner, who was some sort of railroad tycoon who lived like a hermit. He gave himself a heart attack trying to save the contents of the house along with my great-grandfather, the caretaker, the only member of the staff who hadn't gone to town for the fireworks. Most of what the two of them managed to salvage—paintings, jewelry, silver—was shipped to the relatives in Rhode Island. But none of the relatives wanted the statue, so my great-grandfather brought it home to Lowell Mills. Aunt Kate gave it to me as a wedding present."

"I guess that explains why you want it around."

"But your friend Rick may never come around again."

"He'll get over it. My husband was one-quarter Wampanoag, and a statue like that wouldn't have bothered him. He'd have used the thing as a coatrack. Come to think of it, that's not a bad idea, Jessica. You can get some use out of it."

"One of the most important pieces of Americana in my collection, and you want to cover it up under a bunch of ski jackets?" Jessica sighed as she tossed Nancy's windbreaker over Lady Hiawatha's broken arrow quiver. "Well, maybe it's for the best."

Chapter Eight

Jessica was back in Boston before the rush hour traffic turned to molasses. Except for the set-to with her new neighbor, the day had been a success. The shop was taking shape before her eyes. Most of all, it had been fun. Max was bored by her treasures, so unveiling them to an appreciative audience was exhilarating. Nancy wasn't especially discerning. A souvenir teaspoon from Atlantic City delighted her as much as a Tiffany lamp. But Rick had asked some perceptive questions…well, before the statue fiasco. And she'd enjoyed explaining the facets of each artwork.

Maybe that cable interview wouldn't be as scary as she'd thought. Certainly, free publicity wouldn't hurt the shop, especially since she felt hellbent to prove herself to Max as soon as possible by racking up some hefty profits.

She punched Chris's number. As usual, there was no answer. Katy Perry flooded the car with "Roar".

"Hey, it's Chris Bart. I'm on the air or on the road so leave a message and I'll be back to you pronto."

"Chris, I'd love to do the cable show. The shop opens next Tuesday. Looking forward to it so call me back when you can."

Done.

Now there was nothing to do but prepare for the "special night" tomorrow. After all, a tenth wedding anniversary is pretty special. Thank goodness everything was going so smoothly in Boston. Jessica would have felt guilty about leaving Max in the lurch at Stratton Gallery if Eddie hadn't stepped into her shoes so efficiently.

Maybe a little *too* efficiently? The first few days, Eddie pestered her with questions almost hourly: What's the password for the computer? Where is the extra stationery stored? What's the FedEx account number?

But once Eddie had a firm grasp on the all the persnickety business details that Max preferred to ignore, Stratton Gallery appeared to be running at peak performance without Jessica's presence. The lesson, thought Jessica as she parked the car, was that nobody was indispensable. Eddie's presence had certainly been a boon for her own project. She certainly couldn't have devoted so much time to getting Wilder House in shape if she'd been working a full week in Boston too. Yet the fact that she was so easily replaced stung a bit.

Not that Max had been as indelicate as to suggest that Eddie was doing just as good a job, or better, than she'd done. As a matter of fact, they'd barely spoken to each other for weeks. As the opening day for Wilder House grew closer, Jessica's workdays on the Cape grew longer. When she returned from Brewster, often after dark, Max was invariably out to dinner with clients. That was clearly Eddie's influence, since introverted Max rarely made social plans on his own. It was probably good for business, but she missed being able to discuss her day with him.

Tonight, however, she was back early enough to arrange a romantic date night. Perhaps at one of those cozy Italian restaurants in the North End? Red-checked tablecloths, sputtering candles jammed into Chianti bottles, a big plate of linguine with clam sauce...

"I'm home, Max," she called as she tossed her sweater over the banister.

"Upstairs, dear," came the response.

In the bedroom, Max was knotting one of the conservative, blue silk ties he favored, his eyes on the mirror. "You just caught me. I'm meeting Eddie, a client, and his lawyer at the Carlton to discuss an estate appraisal. Two superb Sargent portraits, a Winslow Homer beach scene, a major Kensett landscape, and a slew of Mary Cassatt drawings. Real treasures." Max's eyes gleamed. "Eddie made the contact. He reads the obituaries like a ghoul, but I must say it gets results. He contacted the heirs yesterday and set this up."

"Darn, I was hoping for a quiet dinner at Mario's."

"We'll probably have something to eat at the Carlton afterward." Max glanced at his watch. "If you can be ready in ten minutes, you can come along."

"No way." Jessica sighed and pointed to her muddy shoes. "I've been unpacking and gardening all day. I'm filthy and need a bath."

"You certainly have an exciting life out there in the provinces," said Max as he selected a charcoal gray jacket from a closet chockfull of similar gray jackets. He slipped a slim, crocodile wallet into his pocket. "Did you have any trouble getting that junk unloaded?"

"Not really. One of the neighbors helped."

"I suppose he'll expect you to return the favor by playing the banjo at his barn-raising?"

"This is Twenty-first century Cape Cod, not the Little House on the Prairie," said Jessica as she followed him downstairs. "Just don't let Eddie set up any business dinners for tomorrow night, okay?"

"Tomorrow night? Why not?"

"MAX!"

"Oh, you mean that little matter of our anniversary?"

"Yes, that's exactly what I mean," said Jessica as she straightened his tie a centimeter. "Ten years is serious, and we are going to celebrate."

A horn honked outside, and Jessica parted the curtains. "It's Eddie," she reported.

Max reached for the doorknob, then turned back and reached for Jessica's hand.

"Jessica, I love you," he said in a low voice. "You do know that, don't you? Do you know that I love you?"

The horn sounded again, longer this time.

"Yes, Max, of course I do. Darling…" She stared back at him. His eyes looked almost haunted. "Have I done something that makes you doubt that?"

"No, nothing at all." He dropped her hand and, once again, his eyes were as gray and opaque as his jacket, his pupils like black holes that let no trace of light or emotion escape. "Don't wait up for me. I'll probably be late."

And he was gone.

Jessica leaned against the doorframe and took a deep breath. What brought that on? Max had never been the kind of guy who talked about relationships. And here he was, asking her if she loved him. No, that wasn't it. He asked if she knew that *he* loved *her*. Was he wondering if he loved her?

She was too exhausted to ponder that now.

Tomorrow night, she'd show him just how much she loved him. She made herself a cup of tea and took it to bed. She was asleep before she took the second sip. She didn't hear Max at all when he came in.

Chapter Nine

Soft spring sunlight was streaming through the drapes when Jessica woke the next morning. She looked across the bed. Max wasn't there. His pillow wasn't even dented. The bedside clock read nine o'clock.

"Max?" Jessica tied her pink silk robe at her waist and peered into the bathroom. "Max," she called again at the staircase, a little louder, as she pulled a comb through her hair.

Still no answer. She walked down to the kitchen and saw a note propped up against the espresso machine.

"*Got back after midnight and couldn't bear to wake you. Off to Lenox to evaluate the collection. Back for dinner tonight. Happy Anniversary, M.*"

Well, Max and Eddie must have impressed the heirs last night. From the paintings that Max had mentioned, it sounded like a highly lucrative proposition for the gallery. However, Jessica wasn't certain that Max's mother, the venerable Dierdre Kingsley Stratton, would be too happy about Eddie's hearse-chasing tactics.

She hoped, for Max's sake, that the deceased wasn't a close friend of his mother's. But there was no need to borrow trouble. It was enough that Max was happy. Why on earth had she been so spooked last night by his question? Whether she *knew* he loved her. It was probably normal that he'd feel like he was neglecting her. After all, he hadn't come down to the Cape even once to see the shop. Moreover, he'd probably been feeling pretty neglected himself. She'd been spending almost all her time and energy in Brewster and, whenever she did get back to Boston, she was too tired for anything but a bath, a bite of dinner, and bed. No wonder Max was dining out with clients so often.

Not that she even knew which clients they were, or even what paintings were displayed before the velvet curtains in the front window anymore. She hadn't spent more than five minutes in Stratton Gallery for the past four weeks. The elegant little showroom used to represent their whole life together. They'd been side-by-side for eight hours, five days a week, for over a decade.

Work—when you came down to it, Max's work—gave them all they needed and wanted to talk about. Soon she'd be able to talk about her own gallery as well but tonight, she'd give her husband an anniversary to remember. She poured some milk in her coffee and took it to the pantry.

Yes, there it was, undisturbed, the large box that she'd had delivered last week from a rival antiques house. She slit open the box with the kitchen scissors and spread the crisp tissue paper carefully.

It was even prettier than she remembered. When she first saw the nineteenth-century Pennsylvania quilt hanging in a shop window a few months ago, her heart went pitter-pat. Ten delicate apple-green rosettes on a snowy white background. Ten rosettes. Ten years. It took her all of five seconds to decide to buy it although her hand trembled slightly as she wrote out the hefty check.

"Just get us something that you like," he'd always answer when she hinted for holiday gift suggestions. "I have everything I want."

Over time, Jessica learned that it was true. The things Max liked best *were* the things he already possessed. Like his high-priced English convertible. Like his signet ring and the full rack of silk-twill ties from fancy preppy shops. She'd bought one of the latter, a restrained navy with tiny royal blue dots, as an "if-he-hates-the-quilt" back-up gift. She slid the slim orange box out of its hiding place under a stack of kitchen towels.

Since she was alone in the house, she might as well set the stage for the night's festivities. She bundled the quilt in her arms, placed the tie box on top, and headed up to the bedroom. Swiftly, she stripped the bed and remade it with fresh linen sheets. Once she had draped the quilt over the bed, the room looked cheerful, springlike, and a whole lot less formal.

Next she shook out the ecru lace nightgown and robe that she'd worn on her wedding night. She'd laundered it a few days ago on the Cape since she didn't want Max to see it drying. She fingered a bit of the white satin trim where the jagged rip had been skillfully repaired. A vague feeling of unease made her catch her breath.

That was it. Those words. *Do you know I love you?*

Max had ripped the negligee off her shoulders on their wedding night, demanding that same question over and over again. Max, who was normally so restrained, and almost as shy as she was in the bedroom. The phone rang, shattering her reverie.

"Miz Stratton?" asked an unfamiliar voice.

"Yes?"

"It's Tony da Silva. I got your sign finished. I can put it up this afternoon if you tell me where you want it."

Jessica glanced around the room. There was nothing more to be done here. Everything was ready for tonight. And suddenly, she wanted very badly to be out of the Beacon Hill house.

"Look, why don't you come by early afternoon? I'll drive down this morning, and I'll have the check for you."

"Great. See you around one."

Jessica checked the clock. It was barely ten a.m. She dialed Nancy's office and crossed her fingers. "Nancy, are you free for lunch today?"

Chapter Ten

Jessica was unwrapping two deli sandwiches when Nancy walked in the door.

"Bartender, make mine a double."

Jessica pointed to a six-pack of ginger ale on the counter. "What's up?"

"I've just had my ear talked off for absolutely nothing." Nancy popped open a can and took a long swig. "Some people don't want to buy a house; they just want free therapy."

"Maybe you should start charging them one-hundred dollars an hour."

"Maybe I should. Anything beats real estate these days. Does that sandwich have my name on it?"

"You bet. Extra mustard, no mayo, just as you like it."

"So what's going on?" asked Nancy, pulling up a chair. "I didn't expect you to get down here until Sunday at the earliest."

"I guess I needed some free therapy."

Jessica spoke briskly, but her voice wavered. Nancy looked up from her sandwich.

"This isn't anything about the shop, is it?"

"No, everything's fine on that front."

"Is it Max? Is it something about this anniversary?"

Jessica was silent.

"Bingo. Okay, sweetie, Doctor Webster only has

forty-five minutes for lunch, so let's get started. What's Max done to make you so glum?"

"Nothing."

"I need more than that to go on if you want my expert help."

"The thing is, I don't *know* what's wrong. We hardly talk anymore, and I'm starting to realize that all we ever talked about was running the gallery. He's not showing any interest in this shop, and he doesn't show any interest in me either. He keeps scheduling dinners with clients and forgets to invite me too."

"But isn't that natural? You've been down here most of the time."

"I guess so. I don't know," said Jessica, spreading extra mustard on her own sandwich listlessly. "Last night, he seemed almost *desperate* about something. He looked right at me, and I swear he didn't even see me. He hasn't even touched me since the night I sprung Wilder House on him."

"Maybe he feels rejected since you struck out on your own? Or it could be that he's just plain tired. There used to be two full-time workers at the gallery, and now he's doing it all alone."

"He's not alone. Eddie's hanging around all the time."

"Eddie?" Nancy looked puzzled. "Refresh my memory."

"He worked at the gallery before I did."

"Oh, yeah, Max's old school buddy. You don't like him?"

"I don't like his style. Eddie's the kind of guy who would do anything for a sale."

"What's wrong with that? I could use a guy like

him in my office."

"Nancy!" Jessica frowned. "There's something sneaky and shady about Eddie, but I can't quite put my finger on it. For all the fancy clothes and la-di-dah attitude, he reminds me of the pool sharks who hung around the bars in Lowell Mills. He's part of the problem with Max, but I just don't know how."

"But it's just moonlight and roses for the two of you lovebirds tonight, right? Maybe you should take advantage of that and tell Max how you feel about this guy?"

"Absolutely not! I refuse to think about anyone as obnoxious as Eddie on my anniversary. Tonight, it's going to be Champagne, soft lights, and Max's favorite foods: roast duck, carrots in cream sauce, and *purée de pommes de terre*."

"Pure-what?"

"Mashed potatoes with pretension."

"And I take it you're not planning to sweat over the stove for any of that?"

"C'mon, you know I can't handle anything more complicated than 'heat and serve'. The gourmet shop next to the gallery is delivering everything at seven p.m."

Tony da Silva rapped on the back door and stuck his head in the kitchen. "Miss Stratton? Hello, Nancy." Tony was a 74-year-old retiree who honed his whittling skills and salty verbs in the merchant marine corps. His natural sense of design meant he could be particular about his clients, but any friend of Nancy's got priority and a semi-respectable vocabulary.

"Got your sign out in the truck. Ready to set it up?"

"You bet I'm ready," said Jessica heading for the

door. "I've been waiting for this moment for years."

"Me too," said Nancy as she grabbed her soda.

Tony squatted on the grass as he carefully unwrapped the heavy wooden sign from a cocoon of newspaper and toweling. "So how do you like it?"

Jessica knelt and touched the incised bayberry blue letters with her fingertips. *Wilder House Antiques.*

Nancy whistled appreciatively. "This should draw the crowds."

"Like squirrels to a birdfeeder," said Tony as he rolled up the towels. "I'll get my post-hole digger from out of the truck, and we'll get it planted. Know where you want it?"

"Over there near the hydrangeas?" asked Jessica.

"No way," objected Nancy. "When they're in bloom, they'll block the view. It'll be more visible on the far side of the driveway. I'm going to stand over there and pretend to be a sign. You go over there and see how it looks."

Jessica crossed the street and waved her hand at Nancy. "A little over to the right."

"Like this?"

"No, too far. Two steps to the left."

A dark green jeep pulled up beside her. "Are you setting up a dance class?" asked Rick.

"Nancy's helping me figure out where to put the sign."

"Well, I could see you both from a quarter-mile down the road."

"Then I can stop playing sign?" called Nancy.

Tony walked over to where Nancy was standing. "Looks like a good place to me."

"Can I help you with that?" asked Rick.

"I got it under control," said Tony defensively. "You Mr. Stratton?"

"I'm Rick Martell. Just rented the place across the street.

"What'd I tell you? The sign just pulled in your first tourist."

"Rick's not a tourist, Tony. He's a brand-new Brewster taxpayer who's fully qualified to come to the town meeting with us tonight."

"Not me," said Tony. "I'm off to Boston to pick up that power drill my son-in-law got me."

"Tony, can't that wait until tomorrow?" asked Nancy. "We need every vote if we're going to get this recycling project passed."

"Recycling?" asked Rick. "You mean everyone in town gets together and talks about environmental issues?"

"Mostly they shout," put in Tony. "I usually turn off my hearing aid halfway through."

"You're going, Jessica?" asked Rick.

Jessica shook her head.

"Y'see, Nancy, I'm not the only one playing hooky," hooted Tony.

"She's got an excuse, you old goat. It's her big tenth."

"Tenth what?" asked Rick.

"Wedding anniversary," answered Nancy. "How about you, Rick?"

"You can count on me, Nancy," he said. "You've got at least two votes for recycling tonight."

Chapter Eleven

After a quick ginger-ale toast to Wilder House's new sign, Nancy dashed off to Yarmouthport to show a house. Rick headed home after helping Tony pile the post-hole digger back in his rattletrap pick-up.

As Jessica cleared the lunch dishes, she began to hum a little tune. Here in this tiny country kitchen, with one small paned window over the sink and wooden cabinets that had been painted and repainted so many times that they barely closed, she felt comfortable in proximity to pots and pans for the first time in ten years.

Her Beacon Hill kitchen boasted more marble surfaces than an upscale graveyard. Graveyard was the right image too, since just about everything she'd tried to cook on the imported Aga oven had been stillborn or burnt to a crisp. She'd even made a hash out of Aunt Kate's tried and true corned beef hash during the early days of her marriage. Luckily, Max hated hash, so she'd never bothered to attempt the recipe again.

But even though they survived on take-out when they dined at home, handling the fragile, gilt-edged porcelain plates that Max insisted on for every single meal never failed to give her a twinge of anxiety. Using the simple, mismatched dishes that she stored on the Cape was a relief. This, however, they seemed more mismatched than usual. Evidently, the last clients had broken quite a few of the dinner plates and had replaced the broken items with an extremely ugly pink rose pattern.

However, she did have a box of utterly gorgeous Fiesta Ware which would look terrific in the kitchen. The brightly colored WWII pottery had become so popular in recent years that it would fly off the shelves as soon as she put it up for sale. But why not *use* it first? Why not get a little pleasure from the treasures she'd bought and kept boxed-up for years? Of course, it couldn't become a long-term policy. She'd never make any profits if she ate into her inventory like that. On the other hand, she was sure that today's deli sandwiches would have tasted a whole lot better if they'd been served on the Fiesta Ware. She located the box, which had been pushed under a display case in the front room, and carried it to the kitchen.

"Why is the top shelf bare?" she asked herself a minute later. "Those last renters must have been awfully short." To make room for the Fiesta Ware, she picked up a stack of the ugly pink dinner plates and reached up on tiptoe to store them out of sight on the top shelf. As she did, the top shelf gave a tremendous wobble. Shelf and plates came tumbling down, knocking Jessica to the floor.

"Damn it!" Four of the ugly dinner plates lay smashed at her side—no great loss—although the fifth, miraculously unharmed, lay cushioned in her lap. The shelf itself, after having smacked Jessica's forehead, had managed to clip a jar of cranberry preserves on its downward trajectory. The jam now lay in a puddle of splintered glass, oozing dark red goo over the floorboards and shattered plates.

By the time the mess was mopped up, the throbbing in Jessica's temple had blossomed into a blinding headache that sent her rummaging through the medicine cabinet in search of aspirin. She gulped down two of the crumbling, dusty morsels she found and tried to force herself to think clearly.

She felt too shaky to drive to Boston right away. It would be safer to lie down for an hour and recoup. If she left the house by 4:30, and the traffic was light, she'd still be in Boston by the time the food was delivered. There goes my shower, shampoo, and manicure, she thought miserably as she held a washcloth under cold water and wrung it dry. Thank goodness she'd remembered to put the Champagne in the fridge this morning. Everything in Boston was under control. Retreating to the bedroom, she set the electric alarm clock for 4:15, put the cloth over her eyes, and drifted into deep, dreamless sleep.

Boom!

Jessica woke up with a start. Something was wrong. The room was practically dark, and a heavy rain was pounding on the roof. It wasn't an alarm that roused her, it was *thunder*. Jessica reached for the light switch. Nothing.

By the somber glow from the window, she strained her eyes to read her wristwatch. Eight o'clock? She ran out of the darkened bedroom and bumped into a bureau on the way, scraping the skin on her leg. In the kitchen, she fumbled for a match and a candle and dialed Stratton Gallery. No answer.

Then she tried Max's mobile. No answer there either, but that wasn't a big surprise. Max loathed cell phones and, unless he was out of town, generally kept his own switched off. Was he already home? No. There was no answer on the house landline either.

She'd have to call him from the road. There was no other solution. Jessica pulled on her shoes and dashed to the driveway, clutching her umbrella. At least the rain had started to let up. It was barely a drizzle now. "Finally! One piece of good news," thought Jessica as she turned the key in the ignition. Unfortunately, the storm had turned the far corner of the driveway into a swamp.

The back wheels spun, spewing chunks of mud in every direction. In frustration, she gunned the engine as hard as she could. "Stupid, stupid, STUPID!" she muttered hopelessly as the overpowering stench of gasoline filled the car.

She needed help, and she needed it bad. Her do-gooder neighbor was, of course, off at the Town Meeting. So was everyone else she knew on Cape Cod.

Jessica got out and tried to push the car for another fifteen minutes with no results. Her headache was returning, her bruised shin felt stiff and sore, her shoulders ached, her sneakers were caked with cold, wet glop…and she was ravenously hungry.

What else could go wrong? Limping back to house, she reached for her phone…and it wasn't there. It must have slipped out of her pocket into that dark morass of pebbles and mud. There was no way she was going to drive to Boston now. Shuffling out of her ruined shoes, she dialed Max on the landline. This time, it picked up on the third ring.

"Is that you, Jessica? Where are you?" Max's cool, concerned voice brought a lump to Jessica's throat. Oh, to be in Boston…warm, dry, maybe even a fire in the fireplace on this cold, rainy night. Enjoying a candlelight dinner…snuggling under the new quilt…

Jessica swallowed hard. "I'm still on the Cape. I'm stuck."

"This is an awful connection, Jessica. Did you say you're sick?"

"I said I'm STUCK! My car's stuck in the mud, and it won't budge." Fabulous way to start a romantic anniversary, she chided herself. I'm yelling at my husband and none of this is his fault.

"Calm down, dear." Max's slow, amused voice crackled over the bad connection. "Spend the night down on the Cape, and things will look brighter in the morning."

"It's our anniversary, remember?"

"So that's why I found a found a dead duck on the doorstep."

"That was our anniversary dinner," she whispered.

"It's probably for the best, Jessica." Max's voice sounded strained. "Frankly, I'm pretty burned out myself. The Lenox sale is going to be more complex than I expected. Eddie just dropped off the paperwork and since our evening's postponed, we may as well get started on it tonight. Then I intend to crawl into bed and forget that today ever happened. I suggest you do the same."

"Oh, Max." He always sounded so sensible when she was most upset. "I'm so sorry."

"There's nothing to be sorry about. I better get back to Eddie before he drinks up all the Scotch. Get some rest, and we'll talk in the morning."

"Happ—" Jessica was talking to the dial tone.

The lights flickered back on as she examined the

fridge which was almost bare. There were a few slices of wheat bread, curling with age, and a little jar of peanut butter. The cranberry jam that would have made a sandwich out of these paltry ingredients was history.

If only she could call someone to come over. Or maybe go out for a pizza. But everyone she knew was at that damn Town Meeting. Everyone she knew except...

Her fingers trembled as she dialed the da Silva residence.

"Hello?" A female voice sounded wary.

"Is Tony in, Mrs. da Silva? This is Jessica Stratton."

"Is there something wrong with the sign?"

"No, it's perfect. I heard him say he was going to Boston tonight. My car's broken down, and I wondered if I could have a ride."

"Let me see if I can catch him. He's been dead set on getting that drill tonight, but I wasn't going to let him drive with all that rain pouring down."

Jessica held on to the line for what seemed to be an eternity. Finally Maria da Silva came back to the phone. "Okay, you got yourself a ride. Tony will be over to your place in ten minutes. Though if you want to ride all the way to Boston in that nasty old pick-up, you must be really desperate."

"I am desperate. You see, it's my wedding anniversary tonight."

The voice on the other end softened. "Well then, congratulations. Try and make sure Tony pays attention to the speed limits though. He drives that truck like it's a race car."

Five minutes later, Tony's headlights shone in

front of the house.

"Let's see what's going on with this car," he said, turning his flashlight on the ruts. "Yep, you're stuck pretty deep. That car isn't going anywhere tonight."

"I'll take the bus down on Monday and worry about it then. I'm just so happy to have this ride. I thought my night was ruined."

After twenty minutes, Jessica understood what Maria da Silva meant about speed limits. Tony simply ignored them. His phone was out of juice, but he kept the radio blaring to make up for it. Luckily, there was no traffic and Tony deposited a shaken but grateful Jessica on her Boston doorstep in a record one hour and forty minutes.

The house was quiet, and all the lights were out as she entered the hallway. She noticed a florist's box, the kind that held long-stem roses, on the dining room table. Max hadn't forgotten, had he? She knew the florist always kept the stems wet with a tiny plastic vial. She'd open them and read the card tomorrow. An empty bottle of Moet & Chandon champagne stood on the sideboard. At least one of them had toasted the anniversary in style.

She slipped off her loafers and tiptoed up the stairs. A few rays of soft moonlight filtered through the heavy bedroom curtains. She could dimly make out the pattern of the green-and-white quilt spread over the bed. "I wonder if Max liked it," she thought to herself. "I wonder if Max noticed it," she corrected herself with a smile. A wave of affection for this attractive and enigmatic man she'd married filled her heart.

She crossed the room gingerly in the dark. Clothes seemed to be strewn all over the place. Max must have been very, very tired because he was usually extremely fussy about his clothes. Tired or *drunk,* she wondered as her foot sent a second empty bottle of champagne careening across the carpet.

"Max," she whispered as she pulled back the covers.

"Jessica, what an unexpected surprise!" Eddie's voice held both challenge and satisfaction. Max, wrapped in Eddie's arms, stared at Jessica in horror.

Chapter Twelve

Nancy rapped at the door of Wilder House, feeling worried and a little foolish at the same time. It was nearly noon, Sunday morning, and the day promised to be fine. The foggy morning haze had burned off, and a trace of salt air blew in from the bay.

The tourist season, which would go into full swing after Memorial Day, was heating up. The road traffic in the small colony of Brewster had already doubled. In church this morning, space was at a premium for the first time in months. Nancy wondered what the pastor would say if she suggested reserved seating.

On the way home from Shauna Kelly's birthday party last night, Melanie insisted that she'd seen the lights on in Wilder House. It was probably just a reflection from the headlights, Nancy told her, but she decided to check it out in the morning. And sure enough, there was Jessica's car in the driveway, looking like it had gone ten rounds in an Olympic mud-wrestling final and lost.

She rapped on the door again, more forcefully this time. No answer. Could something have happened to her? Not likely. Perhaps Jessica had finally convinced that stuck-up husband of hers to come and see the shop. Maybe they were out for a walk? Or they'd driven off in his car? Still, it wasn't like Jessica not to check in with her.

Nancy rummaged through her purse for the spare key. She opened the door and peeked in. Several half-filled coffee cups littered the usually spotless front salon. Automatically, Nancy began picking up the cups and carrying them to the kitchen.

"Jessica," she called tentatively. The house seemed dead. All the curtains were pulled, giving a close, gloomy feeling to the room.

"Who's there?" came a hoarse, anxious voice from upstairs.

"Is that you, Jessica? Sorry to break in like this, but I got worried when I saw…"

Nancy's words died on her lips as her friend came down the stairs. Jessica's hair was matted and tangled. A pale blue dressing gown, buttoned wrongly, had almost slipped off one shoulder. The eyes that looked back at Nancy were so red and swollen that Nancy's motherly heart nearly broke. She ran across the room and threw her arms around Jessica.

"There, there, honey. Nancy's here now. It's all right."

The sound of the soft, warm voice started the tears flowing again, and Jessica collapsed into Nancy's arms. Nancy guided her gently to the sofa and, laying Jessica's trembling head on her shoulder, waited patiently until her friend was able to speak.

Jessica, through her tears, wondered how she could even begin to explain things to Nancy. Her mind kept turning and returning to the scene in the moonlit Beacon Hill bedroom. The malicious, triumphant glint in Eddie's eyes. Sleepiness turning to horror on Max's face.

And the horrible, sickening feeling that she should

have known all along.

Dimly, she remembered repeating the word 'no' over and over again as she ran from the room. Max's voice shouting "Jessica, come back, Jessica, come back" as she stumbled down the stairs. Finding her shoes, grabbing her purse...how did she manage to do all that? Running out to the street, walking in the rain, walking all the way to the bus station. Cape Cod, she kept thinking, Cape Cod. Buying a bus ticket. Waiting in the terminal. The taxi to Brewster from the Greyhound depot in Hyannis. All in a daze.

She didn't start crying until she crossed the threshold of Wilder House and disconnected the landline which was ringing off the hook.

Only then did the anguish overflow, nourished by ten years of aching jealousy that she'd felt every time Max and Eddie were together. All those mystifying private jokes that kept them giggling like mischievous schoolboys. All those endless, and utterly boring, reminiscences about prep school parties, skiing holidays in the Alps, scuba diving in the Bahamas, Mediterranean yachts, and fancy charity galas. Some of it just seemed like the price she had to pay for marrying "up". After all, Max would have been equally at a loss at the bowling alley in her home town, especially when the conversation got around to the finer points of used cars, trailer parks, and food stamps.

But to discover that her whole marriage was a smokescreen? A cover-up for Max and Eddie's true love? *And why*? Why couldn't they just be *honest* about it? Probably because it was so much more fun to laugh about it behind poor, stupid, back-street Jessica's back. Laughing at her all the time while they went on about...

This unfinished thought made her sit up straight, eyes blazing with fury, before slumping back into the cushions with an expression of defeat and fatigue.

Nancy took stock of the practical. "Whatever's going on, no sleep and no food aren't doing you any good. Wash up, and we'll find ourselves a proper lunch."

As soon as Nancy heard the water running in the upstairs bathroom, she began straightening up the room, opening the windows and letting the clean spring breeze sweep through the house. She plugged in the landline and, after that, she called Melanie on her own phone and canceled an afternoon appointment with a client.

When Jessica came downstairs into the sunlit living room with her face washed and her hair combed for the first time in days, her spirits lifted in spite of the recent events. As the women drove to the Brewster Coffee Shop, Nancy chattered cheerfully about the Town Meeting, as instinct told her Jessica still needed some distance from whatever was troubling her.

It wasn't until the waitress cleared the lunch dishes that Jessica began her story. Nancy listened without saying a word, eyes fixed on the tabletop. She wasn't sure of her own acting skills, so she didn't look directly at Jessica. Other peoples' sexual lives were other peoples' private business, but frankly, this revelation about Max didn't surprise her that much. It felt more like the missing piece of the jigsaw puzzle. What Jessica described as a "marriage" always sounded more like a boss/employee relationship to Nancy.

So Max was into men? Well, the poor guy sure had bad timing, letting Jessica find out on their anniversary. But then, Nancy reasoned, he'd had no idea that Jessica was going to show up, did he?

"What do I do now?" Jessica asked after a long pause. "I've been living a lie for ten years."

"Have you talked to him?"

"No." Jessica smacked her fist on the table with enough force to make the ketchup bottle rattle. Two teenage boys in paint-stained Red Sox sweatshirts put down their hotdogs and looked over with interest. Nancy laid her hand gently over Jessica's.

"Jessica…"

"What is he going to say to me? That it never happened?" Jessica lowered her voice. "That he wasn't in bed with that snake? Nancy, I *saw* them together."

A waitress ambled through the room with a pot of coffee, but Nancy waved her away.

"Someday, you two are going to have to talk and sort things out." Seeing Jessica's agonized expression, Nancy added softly, "But someday doesn't mean today. At least you've got a place to stay. Do you have everything you need? Clothes, toothpaste, whatever?"

"Enough to get by. But what am I going to do?"

"For starters, you're going to open a very successful antique shop in less than 48 hours. So why don't you come to my place and spend the rest of the day chilling out? Melanie just got a new bikini and she's determined to get a head start on her suntan. She'll be delighted to have company on a great day like today."

Chapter Thirteen

Twenty minutes later, Jessica was reclining in one of Nancy's striped canvas lawn chairs, a glass of iced lemonade at her side. Melanie sprawled on a beach towel, her nose buried in a stack of National Geographic magazines. The soft, scratchy rap that filtered through her headphones sounded like the drowsy buzz of crickets on a warm summer night. In a few minutes, Jessica was fast asleep.

"Just what the doctor ordered," thought Nancy as she surveyed the scene from her kitchen window. Four hours later, Melanie gently tapped Jessica's shoulder and told her that dinner was ready.

"What an awful guest I've been! Sacked out in the backyard like a lawn potato," said Jessica apologetically as she entered the kitchen.

"Let's make that 'easily entertained', which is my favorite kind of house guest," said Nancy as she pulled a casserole dish from the oven. "Melanie, if you'll toss the salad, we'll get this show on the road."

"It smells delicious," said Jessica.

"It's just old-fashioned baked beans," said Nancy. "The secret recipe is brown sugar and molasses."

"Last week you said the secret recipe was onions and ketchup," remarked Melanie.

"Who says my secrets can't change, kiddo?"

Whenever she was with Nancy and Melanie, who

teased each other like sisters, Jessica wondered if she'd have developed a relationship like that with her own mother. Aunt Kate, who kindly adopted Jessica after her parents died, was pushing seventy when eight-year-old Jessica moved in. Kate Paquette remembered things that had happened fifty years ago…and things that happened five minutes ago…but not a whole lot of what went on between. There hadn't been much scope for banter.

Melanie had pulled a pair of oversize jeans and an extra-large sweatshirt over her red-checked bikini. Giant-sized clothes had replaced the black leggings and cropped sweaters she'd worn the last time Jessica visited. Melanie's interests mutated as quickly as her wardrobe. The gymnastics phase had been followed by a guitar phase which morphed into a figure-skating phase. Plus a short but memorable "home-made beauty product" phase during which she'd managed to dye her hair eggplant-purple.

"What's up with the National Geographics?" asked Jessica as she helped herself to salad.

"At long last, Melanie has become an environmentalist."

"C'mon Mom, I was *always* concerned about the future of our planet."

"But so much *more* concerned since Rick Martell gave that ecology talk last week," added Nancy.

"Rick Martell's a teacher?" asked Jessica.

"He's got some sort of research grant at the Woods Hole Oceanographic Institute, but he volunteers for some after-school science activities. They've been very successful."

"He makes 'Save the Whales' totally sexy,"

confided Melanie.

"That guy could make 'Save the Squirrels' sound sexy to you," said Nancy. "As you've probably figured out, Jessica, Rick's the flavor of the month at Nauset High School."

"Like you'd have to be a zombie not to notice he's the hottest guy in town," retorted Melanie. "That killer torso, those dreamy eyes, that gorgeous hair, and the way he wears those jeans. Plus cowboy boots. Do I have to spell it out?"

"At the town meeting, he swept Polly Ford right off her feet. You know how she never likes anyone to speak out of turn, and there he is, a ponytailed newbie, and she lets him take the floor."

"You're kidding!"

"I think he cast a spell on her. He's really impressed with the 'pay as you dump' scheme we have in Brewster, and he wants to take it to Off Cape, to places with landfills."

"Rick says landfills aren't on option on Cape Cod given our fragile water table," interrupted Melanie.

"Good girl, Melanie."

"Soooo…" said Melanie, with a sidelong glance at Nancy as she pushed the last two beans across her plate with a knife, "does that mean I can take his nature classes this summer?"

"We don't know for sure that he's giving nature classes, sweetie. He just mentioned the possibility at the Town Meeting."

"You said that the man from Nickerson State Park was interested."

"And I thought you were interested in saving up for next year's whacko wardrobe. What kind of summer job is going to give you time off for bird-watching?"

Jessica cleared her throat. "Actually, I was planning to ask Melanie if she could help out at Wilder House this summer. I'm sure I could schedule her hours between classes."

"See Mom, that'll be perfect! And I'll have tons of babysitting from Mrs. Carter in August. She emailed me yesterday."

"Why am I always the last to know anything around here?" asked Nancy

"Because there are only two of us around here," said Melanie. "Mind if I skip dessert? Then you two can gossip about me in total privacy."

"Git, you conceited thing. We've got better things than you to discuss."

"She's a great kid," said Jessica, after Melanie stacked the dinner dishes in the sink and left the room.

"You'll get no argument from me on that," said Nancy. She brought the teapot and a plate of cookies to the table. "But that kid is going to be sixteen next month. That's almost a woman."

"That's what I feel like," said Jessica sadly. "Almost a woman."

"What on earth is THAT supposed to mean?"

"C'mon, why did Max marry a poor outsider like me when he had his pick of all the debutantes on the East Coast? Because everyone in Boston society knew about him and Eddie. Everyone but stupid little Jessica."

"Jessica, you're not stupid…"

"I wasn't smart enough to realize that I was window-dressing, was I?"

Nancy busied herself with the tea strainer. "You

were more than window-dressing. You've got history with Max. You were together for ten years."

"Yes, but he's known Eddie ever since he was twelve. That adds up to a whole lot more history."

"Well, at least you know the whole story now. That's better than not knowing, isn't it?"

"That's one way of looking at it."

"It's the only way of looking at it, and don't forget, you've got friends to help you through this. In fact, there's a fold-out couch in the living room if you don't want to be alone tonight."

Jessica shook her head. "If this shop is going to open on schedule, I need to get an early start tomorrow. Could you give me a lift back? I'll be fine. I promise."

"I'll be fine," repeated Jessica to herself twenty minutes later as she waved goodbye to Nancy and turned the key in Wilder House's front door. "I'm definitely going to be fine."

She switched on the lights and sank into the sofa, exhausted again despite her four-hour nap. Maybe she should have stayed with Nancy and Melanie, shielded from her gloomy thoughts by their matter-of-fact cheeriness.

"I'll be fine just as long as I don't think about Max," she thought. "He lied to me, he played me for a fool, but I'm not going to cry about it. Not anymore." She curled into a ball, gripping a throw-pillow tightly to her chest.

The landline rang. Drat. Nancy must have plugged it in while she was straightening up. She stared at it and felt her spine stiffen with apprehension. It had to be Max. Was she ready to speak to him? Nancy was right. She'd have to talk to him sometime. She picked up the receiver, and held it at arm's length for a few seconds, as though it might burn her.

"Jessica!"

There was such genuine relief in Max's voice that Jessica's heart caught in her throat. Pride made her answer brusquely.

"What do you want?"

"Jessica, darling, I just want to talk to you. To try and explain. To know you're all right."

"Nothing's all right. I come home and find you and that…that…"

"Stop, Jessica! Please! That was never meant to happen. You know I would never hurt you."

"I don't know that. Not anymore."

"Jessica, please! May I see you? We need to talk about this face to face. I'll drive down tomorrow and…"

"NO!"

"No," she added more quietly a few seconds later. "I just need some time by myself."

There was silence on the other end of the line.

"Whatever you want," said Max. "Take some time, and then we'll talk."

"Yes," she answered flatly.

"If I can send anything, if you need anything…"

"…I'll call you if I do," said Jessica. "Goodnight, Max."

"Jessica, I …love…you."

A few days ago, she'd answered automatically "I love you too." But now? What did she feel now? Her mind raced back to the scene in the Beacon Hill bedroom. "And what about Eddie?" she asked. "Do you love Eddie too?"

She hung up the phone and switched off the lights.

Chapter Fourteen

The alarm clock buzzed at 8 a.m., rousing Jessica from deep, dreamless sleep. Lying on her back, she rubbed the sleep from her eyes, then reached for the ceiling, stretching luxuriously. Pale morning sunlight trickled through the dotted-Swiss curtains, making the square-cut diamond on her engagement ring glitter against the burnished gold of her wedding band.

Deliberately, for the first time in ten years, she slipped both of the rings from her finger. What did these tiny scraps of metal and compressed carbon really signify? *Jessica and Max Forever* as the ornately lettered engraving claimed? Not likely. She started to slip them back on her finger, then hesitated. Did they really belong on her hand anymore? No. Of course they didn't. She reached across the pillows and dropped them into the top drawer of the nightstand.

But that tiny rush of bravado was followed by a sensation of queasiness. Where was she supposed to go from here? Sliding back into her comfortable life as the deluded paper doll wife was not an option. For years, she'd battled with her jealousy of those elegant society ladies who flocked to the gallery and spent too much time batting their eyes at Max and gushing a little too enthusiastically over Hudson River landscape paintings.

And for years, her self-esteem had been boosted by the fact that Max showed absolutely no interest in their flirtatious attitudes. Would it have been any easier if he'd cheated on her with one of those self-assured, finishing school debutantes instead of Eddie? Probably not. Cheating was cheating.

But it wouldn't have been quite so embarrassing, would it? With Eddie, Max had been having an affair for years, right under her nose. Damn it, Eddie would have been the best man at her wedding if he hadn't managed to break his leg in Bangkok the week before! Now it all made terrible, creepy sense. All the inside jokes. All the little ways that Eddie managed to ridicule and exclude her.

Yes, there was a word for women like Jessica. Beards. She was a heterosexual smoke screen, most likely put in place to hide the real apple of Max's eye from his domineering mother. Well, if Max wanted a slimeball like Eddie, he could have him!

She slammed the nightstand drawer shut, then leapt out of bed and headed for the bathroom. Turning the water as hot as she could stand, she lathered her hair with lemon-scented shampoo, then dried herself hastily. No more tedious sessions with the blow-dryer, making sure her hair was pencil straight. From now on, if her hair wanted to wave or frizz, she wasn't getting in its way. She pulled on her ancient jeans, a faded blue work shirt, and was surprised to realize how hungry she was.

In the kitchen, she lit the stove and placed a pan of water on the burner to make a mug of instant coffee. She opened the fridge expectantly. Nothing. Bare as Mother Hubbard's cupboard. A few crusts of museum quality wheat bread had curled up into a stack of brittle, beige shingles. She tried to bite into one of them but gave up after the first tooth-jarring attempt.

"The problem with country life," she muttered as she tied her sneakers, "is the lack of corner delis." She'd have to drive over to the General Store for muffins. Oh yeah, the General Store. Where the owner's wife, who moonlit as a jewelry designer, would immediately notice that Jessica wasn't wearing that humongous diamond ring this morning. She sure didn't need to be the star of all that village drama before breakfast.

Once she'd slipped the rings back on, grabbed her purse and locked the door, there was another problem.

Transport.

Her car wasn't going anywhere. Friday night's gooey mud had baked into solid brick over the sunny weekend. One good thing: her cellphone wasn't completely buried. She dug it out with the edge of her house key.

Excavating the car, however, was going to take more than a house key. The back wheels were embedded halfway to the hubcaps. What she needed was a shovel. Jessica had never needed to explore the small tool shed on the back lawn until now. She pushed the door open and brushed aside the thick cobwebs that hung from the rafters.

A weak ray of sunlight from the crescent window illuminated a shelf of rusted paint cans, cardboard boxes filled with rags, old newspapers, and dusty bottles of turpentine and brass cleaner. She discovered a shovel with a slightly warped wooden handle hanging on a nail on the far wall.

Digging out the car proved to be no small task. Ten minutes later, the faint mist of perspiration on Jessica's forehead was developing into an honest sweat and she'd only managed to chip two measly clumps of dirt away from the rear left tire.

She didn't notice the dark green jeep that had pulled into her driveway until she heard the sound of a sympathetic, yet not entirely unfamiliar, voice.

"Are you planting that car or burying it?" asked Rick.

"Can't you tell I'm trying to harvest it?"

At this, Rick burst into a peal of laughter so engaging that Jessica found herself laughing as well.

"Mind if I take a look?" Rick squatted near the back wheels and felt the earth that Jessica had dug up. Perfect white teeth contrasted his wind-tanned skin when he smiled. As before, his thick, dark hair was tied back with a leather band.

"I wasn't sure if I should be digging in front of the wheels or in back of them," began Jessica helplessly.

"You were on the right track. Let me give it a try." Rick took the shovel from her and with a few swift, even strokes, he freed both back and front wheels. "That should do it. Start the engine, and I'll give you a push."

"I hate to cause you all this trouble," said Jessica. "First you protect my homestead, then you unload the van for me, and now…"

"It's no trouble. I'm just being neighborly."

"I shouldn't let you but…" Really, this man was impossible to resist, especially when he smiled like that. Maybe Nancy was right. Maybe he did cast spells on women.

Rick watched closely as Jessica settled into the driver's seat, her sun-dried blonde hair flouncing like windswept fields of golden wheat…so different from

Martine's sleekly styled cap of raven curls that demanded weekly appointments at upscale salons. Martine wouldn't have been caught dead in a casual denim shirt with a paint stain on the collar like Jessica's. Martine favored carefully chosen designer ensembles that were packed off to the dry cleaner five minutes after being worn. These women were completely different except for one very important thing.

They both wore wedding rings. And that meant…

"Rick?" Jessica, jingling the car keys, broke his reverie. "Are you sure I shouldn't get out and help push?"

"No way. Get the motor running, and we'll be in business."

After several thrusts, the sedan shuddered and pulled free. As Jessica climbed out of the car, Rick was already busy with the shovel filling in the deep holes in the driveway.

"Rick, you've saved my day again."

"No thanks are necessary, milady," he answered, bowing over the shovel as though it was a knight's sword. "Feel free to call on me whenever you get stuck in a rut."

"Could I at least offer you some coffee before you go?" Oops, she hoped he didn't mind instant coffee as much as Nancy did. *Did she have any milk though? Any milk that hadn't turned sour? The carton that Nancy brought was several weeks old…*

"That's tempting, but I thought you said you were in a hurry."

"Oh, I was just going to the grocery store."

"What a coincidence," said Rick. "So am I." He opened the passenger door of the jeep. "Let's save energy and carpool."

Chapter Fifteen

If a man's car mirrors his personality, what have we here? Jessica looked around the cluttered jeep. Max kept his immaculate blue-gray import in a Boston garage near the gallery. The red leather interior still looked like new, largely because Max refused to transport any paintings or antiques in it, even in the trunk. He always borrowed Jessica's sedan for work.

Rick's jeep, on the other hand, looked like a mobile junkyard. He'd hastily tossed a pile of computer printouts onto the back seat to make room for Jessica. They landed on a sack of topsoil, a rolled-up plaid blanket, a set of barbells, a toolkit, a wicker basket, and a pair of battered track shoes. As Jessica groped for the seatbelt, she came up with a handful of sharp, rock-hard yellow granules.

"Cracked corn," explained Rick. "Quail love it."

Hmmm. Max loved quail too. He liked his quail stuffed with *foie gras* and served with brandy sauce at *Chez Ghizlane*. No, forget about that! From now on, she wasn't going to define anything she heard about in terms of what Max liked or disliked. "Are there lots of quail around here?" she asked.

"Not as many as fifty years ago, but there's a whole family in the woods behind my house. I bought a five-pound sack a few days ago, but the bag got caught on the tire jack. Result: one pound of corn gone to the birds and four pounds of corn in the car."

"I've never seen any quail. I've hardly spent any time here."

"Don't worry. You'll see loads of them if you're spending all summer here."

"I guess I will." She looked up in alarm as the jeep sped past the General Store. "Hey, where are you going?"

"You were headed for the General Store?" asked Rick in surprise.

"Of course. Where are you going?"

"To the supermarket in Orleans."

Jessica looked blank.

"You mean, you don't know where the supermarket is?" Rick whistled. "You buy all your food at postcard places with tourist markups? Boy, you really don't know the Cape. Allow me to serve as your shopping guide."

Jessica laughed. "That would be delightful. And in return for all these favors, it would give me great pleasure to invite you to dinner tonight. That is, if you're not doing anything."

"No, I'm free, but it's not necessary."

"After all you've done for me, of course it is."

"Then I'd be honored."

Rick did indeed prove to be an excellent guide, and by the time they reached Orleans, Jessica knew a whole lot about cranberry bogs, including the ones that were "de-evolving" into natural wetlands.

As soon as they walked through the sliding glass doors of the supermarket, Jessica realized the enormity of her folly. When she'd blithely invited Rick to dinner, she'd been laboring under the delusion that the offer would entail a call to her usual Boston caterer and ordering the *plat du jour* for two. Here she was, looking at acres of potatoes, celery, cabbages, and all sorts of stuff that would require boiling, broiling, or baking if they were going to resemble anything that looked like dinner.

"Is there something wrong?" asked Rick.

"No, it's just the size of this place," she said quickly. "It's so much bigger than the grocery shops in the city."

"Yeah, you can run a marathon between the rutabagas and the rigatoni in a place like this. Shall we meet at check-out in, say, thirty minutes?"

As soon as he left, Jessica felt like curling up in fetal position and screaming. Why on earth had she asked him to *dinner*? Why hadn't she simply asked him over for a *drink*? Uncorking a bottle of wine and opening a bag of pretzels was a hostess exercise that she could pull off with panache. Why had she offered him a whole damn *dinner*? "Because it seemed so natural and neighborly at the time," she told herself. "Natural if you know how to cook," a nasty little inner voice answered back.

Her ever-dependable pesto, alas, was out of the question. Her week-old basil seedlings wouldn't make enough sauce for a gerbil on a diet. Could she try to fry some hamburgers? Hamburgers got fried, didn't they? Or were they baked? Jessica wasn't one-hundred percent sure. But burgers would be a no-go if her guest turned out to be a vegetarian. He certainly seemed to have a soft spot for cornfed quail, but maybe he only cared about quail when they were alive. "I'm such an idiot." Jessica sighed. She wandered down one of the center aisles despondently and tossed a can of soup in her cart. Cream of Mushroom, she recalled, had been the essential ingredient in almost all of Aunt Kate's fancier recipes.

Suddenly the temperature fell sharply, and Jessica's spirits rose to the skies.

Frozen food! Two enormous rows! Why hadn't she thought of that?

There was exciting stuff too. Far more glamorous than the TV dinners she'd known back in Lowell Mills. Basted honey teriyaki. Mediterranean lasagna. Braised lamb with coconut sauce. What about broccoli and snap beans in a creamy cheddar sauce? That would cover the vegetarian base. She looked at the instructions on the wrappers. "Boil in the bag." Hell, that was no harder than making tea. Tonight's dinner was going to be a piece of cake…in every sense of the word "cake". Frozen strawberry cheesecake, frozen Red Velvet cupcakes, even apple cobbler. Nope, the picture on the apple cobbler package looked a little too "down home" and boring, even for a specialist in American folk art. Tonight, she'd go all out and exotic. Jessica slid a box of frozen Black Forest cake in the cart.

As she headed for the cash registers, she noticed a stack of macaroni and cheese mixes. That was another one of Aunt Kate's stand-by dinners. Maybe if she felt very Gordon Ramsay-ish someday, she could attempt something as complicated as that. Recklessly, she threw several blue-and-yellow packages into the cart and glanced at the clock on the wall. She'd kept Rick waiting for ten minutes, and she still hadn't paid for anything.

Luckily, he was still in the process of checking out

himself. Jessica watched as he loaded lettuce, onions, mushrooms, and cheeses into a canvas bag. She pulled her cart into a line that was just opening up and waved at him.

"Paper or plastic?" asked the clerk.

"Um, paper, I guess." She noticed that, like Rick, most of the other shoppers had baskets or reusable tote-bags.

"Need any help with those?" asked the bagger a few minutes later as he dropped the last box of macaroni in the second bag.

"Oh no, they're light," said Jessica as she punched in her credit card code. So was the total. The bill was a fraction of what she would have paid her Boston caterer. Bags in hand, she hurried out to the parking lot. The sun was bright, and Rick was rolling the jeep's convertible top down.

"If you don't like the wind in your hair, I'll put it back up. Seeing as the weather's so nice, I thought we could take advantage of the sun."

"That'd be lovely." Jessica dropped the bags in the back and climbed in.

There was no need to talk much on the way back. The blue sky made it clear that spring was here to stay. Last Friday's fierce rain had kickstarted a profusion of delicate wildflowers that lined the road too. It was fantastic to sniff the fresh air and feel the sun soaking into one's bones.

All too soon, Rick was parking the car. "What time should I come over?"

"Eight o'clock?"

"Let me bring the wine. White or red?"

"Gee, I hadn't really decided what's for dinner.

Shrimp in Thai coconut curry sauce with basmati rice? Or Mediterranean-style lasagna?" Jessica wracked her brain to remember her vegetarian option. "Broccoli and mixed vegetables with cheddar cheese sauce," she added triumphantly.

"Any of the above would be fine," said Rick as he extracted the bags from the back of the jeep. "I'd say you're a pretty efficient shopper if you squeezed the makings for all that into two little sacks."

As if on cue, one of the paper bags, soggy from its cargo of frozen food sweating in the sun, burst. Rick knelt to pick up the cartons and exploded with laughter.

"I don't see what's so funny."

"Look at this junk, Jessica. It's not even food. It's a bunch of chemical additives held together by high fructose corn syrup." He picked up the Black Forest cake box and pointed to the rows of tiny gray writing on the side. "Read that and weep. The only natural product you've got here is the cardboard packaging."

"I never claimed to be top chef," she said defensively.

"That's true. You never did." Rick started laughing again, and this time Jessica joined in.

"I don't know what to do about tonight," she said wistfully when she caught her breath. "I've got some macaroni and cheese mix. Is that real enough for you? Or maybe I can take you to a restaurant instead?"

"I've got a better idea. Let me make the dinner."

"Rick, I'd be too embarrassed…"

"It's settled." Rick stacked the lasagna, curry, and cake boxes like so many children's colored plastic blocks and handed them to Jessica. "Eight o'clock."

"But…" Jessica clutched forty-five dollars of

frozen entrées to her heart as Rick turned back to his house. "But Rick, what am I supposed to...?"

"Red," he called over his shoulder. "Make it red wine."

Chapter Sixteen

Rick was slicing onions and peppers on the cutting board and wishing he could kick himself. Why on earth had he invited her for *dinner*? Because it seemed natural and neighborly, he told himself. Yeah, but a simple pre-dinner drink would have been natural and neighborly enough. But now? He was stuck with her for a whole, long evening.

Nothing wrong spending a quiet evening with the girl next door, right?

Yeah, right. Except this one had a whole lot of hardware on her left hand that flashed "Married: Red Alert." He sure didn't need any more drama like that. Not after Martine. Martine had simply "forgotten" to tell him about her oil lobbyist husband back in London, hadn't she? It was just too pathetic to think how hard he'd fallen for her lies and evasions.

No more married women.

Ever.

Not that he could blame himself for letting Jessica sneak into his fantasies. He didn't have X-ray vision, did he? She wore driving gloves the first time they met, and gardening gloves the next. He'd have nipped those first flashes of fantasy in the bud if he'd seen those rings right away.

Or maybe not?

After all, the woman was alone *all the time*, and

that was damned odd. No husband to lift all those heavy boxes? No lover to share all that driving? In fact, whenever she needed anything, nobody but Rick Martell and that real-estate lady showed up to help. For that reason, he'd been ninety-eight percent certain that Jessica Stratton was widowed or divorced...until she'd blithely mentioned her tenth wedding anniversary the other day.

Was this particular penance yet another facet of the Spirit Quest that his sister's healer recommended? Turning his back on a flashy executive position in the oil industry, taking a low-paying research job in an environmental agency, and doing volunteer work in the schools wasn't enough? Now he had to face the fact that the girl-of-his-dreams was right next door and happily married to someone else? If so, this was pretty nasty payback for the Martine debacle which was, at least on his part, purely unintentional adultery.

In spite of that, he couldn't help sneaking admiring glances at Jessica all the way to Orleans today. Windblown hair, no make-up. Come to think of it, he'd never seen Martine without her false eyelashes. Well, yeah. *Once*. The time he'd woken her up swatting at what looked like a massive black spider crawling across the pillow.

He'd learned a whole lot of French swear words that night.

There only was one smart way to deal with the Jessica dilemma: Cut whatever feelings he had off at the pass. Like pulling off a bandage fast. "*So what does your husband do?*" That would be a good way to get the conversation flowing. Or: "*How was the anniversary party?*" He slid the onions into the frying pan. "I know how you feel, boys," he said, watching them wilt in the hot oil.

****

Across the street, Jessica took off the fifth sweater she'd tried on and tossed it onto the massive heap of clothes that was piling up on the bed. This was a simple dinner with a neighbor. It was nothing to get fussed about. But nothing in her limited wardrobe *looked* right. Nothing *felt* right either. She hadn't had so much problem pulling together an outfit in years. At least not since she'd mastered the whole designer "beige-on-beige" bourgeois look that Max's crowd favored.

Now she felt like she was back in high school. Not surprising, especially since most of the clothes in a pile on the bed dated from high school. She rooted through the rejects for the electric-blue V-neck sweater that she'd discarded a few minutes ago. It was colorful and comfortable. With ballet slippers and jeans, it would have to do.

She headed down the stairs and checked the wine-rack in the hall closet.

A Chablis ? Why not?

No, he'd said red. She pulled out a California Cabernet. Nice enough wine…but the guy deserved something better. After all, he'd unloaded the van on that scorching hot day. He dug out her car this morning. And now he was cooking dinner for her. Dimly she remembered that Max had stored a few cartons of extremely expensive French wine in the cellar. He'd even installed a lock on the cellar door to protect the precious bottles while they "aged" to perfection.

Well, that wine was plenty old enough to drink by now. Her expedition to the cellar hit pay dirt too: a dusty carton of outrageously posh Château Margaux. Max didn't think of it as a wine to be enjoyed though. He called it an investment. Well, he would, wouldn't he?

Enough of investments. Enough of Max. She was going to drink that fancy wine tonight, with a perfect stranger, and enjoy every last sip of it. Though she was only going across the street, the air had chilled considerably, so she rummaged in the closet for her mohair shawl. As she draped it over her shoulders, the loose weave snagged on the diamond in her engagement ring.

Cradling the wine bottle in the crook of her arm, she slipped off the ring and awkwardly tried to extricate it from the shawl without pulling the yarn too far. All day long, that damn ring had been bugging her, reminding her of something she'd be better off to forget. Her eyes lit on a jelly jar filled with the nails, screws, and bolts that she'd used to repair the kitchen shelf. Rebelliously, she dropped the engagement ring into the jar and added the wedding band to keep it company.

Feeling loads lighter—but slightly naked—she locked the door behind her.

Chapter Seventeen

Rick's front door swung open when Jessica rapped on it, so she walked right in.

"Rick?"

No answer.

"Rick?"

She looked around. The jeep might have been a rolling junk-heap, but the living room, filled with slightly threadbare upholstered furniture, was admirably neat. A small dinner table near the window was set with candles. The only signs of disorder were the stacks of computer printouts piled up in the corner. A mouthwatering aroma wafted from the back of the house, so Jessica followed her nose to the kitchen.

Rick stood with his back to the kitchen door. "Take Five," a jazz tune she'd always loved, was playing in the background. Rick whistled along with the melody, his broad shoulders and slim hips swaying gently to the beat. There was something so confidently masculine about the way he moved around this domestic scene that Jessica, raised in an all-female household, watched as if entranced. Unless on a quest for ice cubes or martini olives, Max never entered the kitchen at all.

His back still to Jessica, Rick, still whistling, moved to the sink where he rinsed his hands. He turned around in surprise as he dried his hands on a checkered towel. "Hey, Jessica, I didn't hear you come in. How long have you been here?"

"I knocked on the front door, but the drums drowned me out," she said, handing him the wine.

"I always need percussion when I cook. My goodness." Rick studied the label. "Major league Bordeaux, Jessica. Hope the chow can live up to the challenge."

"People who can't cook compensate for our insecurities with fancy wine. Rick, again, I felt so dumb about this morning…"

"Forget it. Why don't you open this serious booze and let it breathe a bit? I think the corkscrew's in the top drawer over there. I'm still not sure where everything is in this house."

"I know the feeling. Every fall, when I close the house after the last renter leaves, the utensils have all migrated to the least logical places," Jessica said as she rummaged through the drawer. "Smells great, by the way. What's cooking?"

"Chili con carne. If you're born and bred in Houston like I was, you need a weekly fix of Texan cooking."

"Is there anything I can do to help?"

"I'm not sure. Just how kitchen-impaired did you say you were?"

"Pretty bad. I even made the worst mud-pies on the playground."

"Then we won't ask for trouble." Rick handed her the salad bowl. "Take this over to the table and look through the CDs for some dinner music."

"Coward," Jessica called over her shoulder as she exited.

So far so good on small talk, thought Rick. This

would be shaping up into a swell first date…if only it were a date, he reminded himself. The last thing I need is to get involved in somebody else's marital mess. Be safe and stick to the plan. And Plan A is "stay cool" and make this a very early evening. In fact, I can start by serving the chili right away instead of letting us dawdle over a drink.

In the living room, Jessica flipped through a large and eclectic collection of CDs. A lot of jazz, a whole bunch of singers with French names that she didn't recognize, and some classical guitar. Tom Waits. Bonnie Raitt. Macy Gray. Ella Fitzgerald. Why not Ella? She was always soothing, and Jessica felt a bit nervous. This almost felt like a date, but no, this could *not* be a date. Given her marital mess, the last thing she needed was an involvement with a man, a man she didn't even know. She slid the disc into the machine and pushed the "play" button. "Let's Fall in Love" blasted from the speakers. She quickly lowered the sound.

"Cole Porter songbook," said Rick, walking in with the wine and two glasses. "Good choice. Why don't you pour us some wine? Dinner will be ready in a minute."

Spotting a box of matches on the mantel, Jessica lit the candles. She'd just finished pouring two glasses of deep, ruby-red Bordeaux when Rick walked in with two heaping plates.

"Rick, this is tremendous!" exclaimed Jessica, staring at her plate. "It looks like something out of a magazine."

"So do you," thought Rick, watching the candlelight throw its sparkling glow across Jessica's face as they sat down. *Time to put Plan A into gear. Time to tell her how much I'm looking forward to meeting this husband of hers. That called for a toast, didn't it?* He raised his glass.

"To you…" he began.

Jessica leaned forward, both hands cupping her wineglass.

"To you and…" *Wait a second! Where was that humongous gem she had on her left-hand ring finger this morning? What kind of crazy game was this woman playing with him?*

"Yes…?" prompted Jessica.

"To you…and to the unexpected," said Rick slowly.

"To unexpected pleasures, at any rate," said Jessica brightly after the pause threatened to become uncomfortable. "Like this marvelous homemade chili. I think the toast should be to the chef." She raised her glass and took a sip.

Plan B. What the hell is Plan B? wondered Rick as he watched her intently. He didn't detect any come-hither in her straightforward gaze. In fact, her smile conveyed nothing except neighborly concern that he might have been struck deaf and dumb all of a sudden. He raised his glass again, took a long swallow, and turned to his plate. Plan B is all hers, he decided.

Chapter Eighteen

That toast was a *total* conversation-killer. Jessica toyed with her salad and cast about for an environmentally appropriate topic that might interest her host. He'd been chatty and charming about cranberry bogs, water tables, and quail in the car this morning. Now he'd gone all silent and broody, staring into his chili bowl as if it were a crystal ball.

"Nancy tells me that you're working at the Woods Hole Institute," she ventured. "Are you an oceanographer?"

"Just a mechanical engineer on a grant. I'm helping out on a robotics project, a drone that follows the tides and tracks offshore pollution."

"I'm impressed."

"You should actually be depressed about it. More than four-hundred pounds of plastic gets dumped in the oceans every second, and we're nowhere near finding a way to clear it up."

"And you're trying to find a solution?"

"I started out in Big Oil as an engineer on off-shore platforms. Then I gave some interviews to a news magazine that pleased the suits, and I got transferred to the Public Relations department. Suddenly I had tons more money, first class travel all over the world, and a fancy company car. It was all good until…"

He paused and refilled the wineglasses.

"Until the day I found myself on a beach with dead seagulls and acres of putrefying fish." Rick shook his head and stared out the window. "My mission was 'damage control', and guess what that meant? Controlling the damage to the international cartel that caused the disaster." He looked back at Jessica. "Is this too heavy for dinner?"

"Not at all. What did you do?"

"Quit. Got in touch with my sister. She fixed me up with a healer who told me that I wouldn't be able to clear my conscience until I'd cleaned up some of the mess I'd made."

"Is that why you're giving the ecology classes?"

"Since the future generation has to cope with the planet that their elders trashed, it seems wise to give them a heads-up."

"Nancy says you'll be teaching summer school as well."

"Good grief, that woman is like a twenty-four-hour news station. If we could harness her energy, we could light up the whole town."

"The whole East Coast," agreed Jessica. "Nancy's the one who's responsible for getting me here for the summer."

"Now that sounds like a more agreeable story, and it's your turn to do some of the entertaining around here."

"My story is not as dramatic as yours. About two months ago…"

"Back up! I was born in Texas, and you were…?"

"…born in a mill town in New Hampshire. My parents died when I was a kid, and my Aunt Kate adopted me. Actually, she was my great aunt."

"She's one who taught you not to cook?"

"But she made me do my homework, and that paid off with a college scholarship. I majored in history, then I got a job in an American Art gallery in Boston, and then I got…" Jessica stopped abruptly.

Rick waited.

"…then I got married."

"Ah."

Now it was Jessica's turn to look out the window. "Goodness. How did I get to Cape Cod? That was your question, right? A few months ago, I was having lunch with Nancy and the idea of opening a boutique came to us—well, it came to Nancy first—and here I am. Ready to open my own Folk Art boutique tomorrow."

"I think you've left out a few chapters," said Rick warily. "You were saying that you got married and…"

"It's awfully cold in here, isn't it?"

"Do you want a sweater?"

"No, I brought a wrap." Jessica stood up and looked across the room. "I had it when I came in."

"Is this it?" Rick picked up the mohair shawl she'd draped over a chair. He wrapped it around her and led her to the sofa. "Are you feeling all right? If you tell me you're deathly allergic to chili peppers and beans, I'll commit culinary hara-kiri with a butter knife."

"The chili is delicious," insisted Jessica. "It's just that I'm so cold all of a sudden. There must be a draft coming down from the chimney."

"I don't feel any draft, but your hands are freezing." Rick started to rub them gently. "Is there something wrong? Can I help?"

Can I help? When was the last time a man had asked her that? This man's hands were so warm, and his voice was so comforting. She had a sneaking suspicion that if he wrapped his arms around her, he'd be able to help her even more. But where would that lead? Down a path she didn't want to tread. Max was a low-down, lying cheater, but Jessica Stratton had principles.

"There's nothing you can do," said Jessica. "I just need to go home."

"Jessica, you don't have to leave."

"No, I have to get back. It was a lovely dinner. Thank you so much."

She opened the door and stepped out before Rick could say another word. If the idea was to get the evening over early, he mused, mission accomplished. As he watched her walk across the lawn, the CD player started up again with "Let's Fall in Love."

"Give it a rest, Ella," said Rick as he carried the barely touched plates to the kitchen. "No takers on that tonight."

Chapter Nineteen

The shrill ring of the landline dragged Jessica out of a deep sleep.

"Wait a minute, wait a minute." She yawned as she slid her feet into her terry slippers.

The phone stopped ringing as soon as she got to the bedroom door.

"Of course," she muttered. She glanced at the clock. 8:20. All the prep for the Wilder House opening had been finished yesterday, so she kicked off her slippers, slouched back into the pillows with a sigh of contentment, and pulled the covers up to her chin.

Seconds later, her cell—miraculously rejuvenated after its mud-bath—started up. She sat up in annoyance and pulled it out of the charger.

"Hey, Jessica! Is that you?"

"Who else answers my phone, Nancy?" The words were half muffled by another yawn. "What's up?"

"Not you, apparently, so it's a good thing I called. Your shop would be getting off to a pretty sorry start if you slept right through your first business day."

"Antique shops don't open at dawn's early light, Nancy. Nobody buys Victorian candlesticks before breakfast."

"Ah." There was silence on the other end of the line. "Sorry, I've been showing a summer cottage to a guy who had to make the 8:25 flight to New York. I had my breakfast a century ago, and I'm in the mood for fancy candlesticks. If I bring some doughnuts, will you open early for me?"

"Chocolate doughnuts?"

"Icing, sprinkles, the works."

"You've got a deal."

Jessica dressed quickly and headed downstairs and drew open the curtains in the front room. Cool, pearly sunlight had already begun to peek through a damp, dewy haze. She looked around in satisfaction. A bevy of nineteenth-century baby dolls waved their bisque porcelain hands at her from their perch atop the bookshelf. Silver candlesticks, gilded mirrors, and brass door-knockers—all polished to perfection—glowed in the early morning sun. Lady Hiawatha, watching over the display cases with her enigmatic Mona Lisa smile from her vantage point in a sunny corner, seemed at home in her surroundings. This shop is good, thought Jessica, this shop is good, and it's all my own.

In contrast, what passed for her personal life back in Boston was a total train wreck. And come to think of it, her personal life wasn't off to a very spectacular start on Cape Cod either. She looked across the street toward Rick's house, and the memory of last night's dining disaster made her cringe. Not really much of a dinner, was it? Three bites of chili, two sips of wine, and she lost control, dashing home before she broke into tears.

Of course, it could have been even worse. One more sip of wine, one more minute sitting next to Rick feeling the gentle touch of his hand over hers, one more kind word from him, and she'd have blurted out the whole sordid saga of her make-believe marriage. And how ghastly it would have been to see the concern in his eyes turn to pity? And what if she'd thrown herself at him as revenge for what Max had done to her?

Running away might have made her look stupid, and it was certainly rude as hell, but that was better than behaving like the pathetic loser she was, up to her neck in abandonment issues.

The lights came on in the living room across the street. She imagined Rick at the dining table. Was he reading the paper? Drinking coffee? Or maybe herbal tea? Was he dressed yet? Or was he still in his bathrobe? Or bare-chested in pajama bottoms? Jessica felt her cheeks redden. This was ridiculous. One thing was sure: Rick Martell wasn't wasting his time staring at her house like a demented voyeur. She pulled the curtains closed with jerky motion. He'd probably written her off for good and was wondering what kind of nuthouse she'd escaped from.

By the time Nancy pulled into the driveway with a box of doughnuts, two Fiesta Ware plates were dusted and waiting on the kitchen counter and the kettle was whistling.

Nancy scowled at the kettle. "Does this mean you're giving me that lousy instant coffee again?" she asked. "You get a client thinking over a pair of those expensive Victorian candlesticks, you need to give them a decent cup of joe."

"Is this 'Pick on Jessica's Kitchen' week or something?"

"Huh? Someone else has been complaining the menu around here?"

"Everybody. Nobody. Forget it." Jessica arranged the doughnuts on a plate. "You want to eat in here or out in the front room?"

"In front, if you don't mind crumbs. I want to be your first customer. Melanie will be sixteen in a few days, and I'd like to get her something with a little more sentimental value than a Grumpy Cat mouse pad."

"Follow me," said Jessica, after dunking her doughnut in her coffee mug and taking a bite. She gestured with her elbow toward the oak claw-foot dining table which was set with an inviting display of pottery and pewter dinnerware. "You haven't seen the place since I put all the merchandise on view. What do you think?"

"Not too shabby," said Nancy as she stood in the doorway. Colorful quilts were draped over the Windsor chairs near the fireplace. The mantels and bookshelves were packed with candlesticks, pouty-faced porcelain dolls in ruffled dresses, doll-house furniture, copper pots, brass knick-knacks, and armies of lead soldiers. Antique mirrors and sepia posters covered the walls.

"Not bad at all," Nancy repeated as she settled herself on the sofa. She picked up a cranberry-colored pitcher from the coffee table and squinted at the sticker on the bottom. "Fifteen? This thing only costs fifteen bucks?"

"No, it's number fifteen. You have to check the price list." Jessica handed her a printed sheet. "That happens to be a fairly rare example of tinted Sandwich glass and it costs $590."

"Melanie doesn't need anything with that much sentimental value." Nancy put the item down with rather more care than when she picked it up. "Do people dicker over the prices in joints like this?"

"The pros always do."

"Then it's just like real estate." Nancy's eyes

brightened. "How's about I offer you $15 for that used pitcher?"

"No way."

"I foresee problems ahead." Nancy got up and wandered through the room, sipping her coffee reflectively. Her eyes lit on Lady Hiawatha. "Maybe I can take that cursed thing off your hands. What's she's going for?"

"Not for sale. Family heirloom, remember?"

"Two strikes. Maybe you better give me a suggestion."

Jessica walked over to a side table. "What about this?" She took an enameled, heart-shaped locket from a showcase. On a glossy ivory background, a bouquet of tiny blue forget-me-nots were tied with a delicate pink bow. The silver filigree clasp was shaped like a seashell.

"It's beautiful," murmured Nancy as she turned it over in her hands.

"Here's the spring." The locket opened at Jessica's touch, revealing two tiny circular frames. "You could put pictures of yourself and her father in it."

"It's perfect," said Nancy. "Does this cost a fortune too?"

"No, it's not very old."

"Neither is Melanie."

Jessica checked the price list. "Forty-eight dollars. But I'd much rather give it to you."

"Nope, I'm buying this fair and square. You say forty-eight? I'll give you forty-five, and that's my final offer."

"Thirty-five and not a penny more," countered Jessica.

"Sold!" Nancy pulled out her checkbook. "Can you gift wrap it?"

Jessica shook her head.

"What a racket you've got here." Nancy uncapped her pen. "You don't open till lunchtime. No gift-wrap. Crummy instant coffee."

"I don't take consumer complaints either. What do I get Melanie for her birthday?"

Nancy looked up from her checkbook and smiled. "How about a rare example of antique tinted Sandwich glass? She can use it as a cooler for her diet soda. Serve taco chips to her pals in it…"

"Seriously, please."

"I'm giving her a doodad with photos of her ancestors. How about a picture frame that she can use for a photo of Chris Hemsworth or Harry Styles?"

"Good idea." Jessica picked up the cherry wood frame on the window-ledge and reopened the curtains. Both women looked up as a dark green jeep backed out of the driveway across the street.

"Stick a snapshot of Rick Martell in that frame, and you'd really make her day."

"I had dinner with him last night."

"With Rick? Do tell!"

"There's nothing to tell."

"Hold on just a minute," called Nancy as she ran back to the kitchen. "This calls for more sugar and carbs." She was back in an instant with a chocolate doughnut. "OK, I'm all ears." Nancy arranged the chintz sofa cushions around her and looked at Jessica expectantly. "Let's have all the juicy details."

"There aren't any juicy details. It was just a dinner. Period."

"Start at the beginning."

Jessica rolled her eyes. "He came over and dug my car out of the mud."

"Damsel in Distress. Hero to the rescue." Nancy rolled her eyes. "A little too rom-com and trite for my taste, but it works. Go on. What happened next?"

"Then he drove me to the grocery store."

"Domestic touch. Very nice."

"Then I asked him over to dinner…"

"You did WHAT?" Nancy looked at Jessica with astonishment. "You? The woman who can barely boil water? What were you planning to feed the poor guy?"

"I had two shopping bags of exotic frozen entrées."

Nancy stifled a giggle.

"OK, he didn't think much of the menu either. So he asked me to dinner."

"To a restaurant?"

"No. His place."

"Ahhh." Nancy licked the sprinkles off the doughnut's icing. "I rented him that joint. One hundred and forty square feet, and almost all of it is master bedroom. Go on."

"He made chili and we were listening to music and having a nice time. Then he proposed a toast, and it got kind of strange." Jessica broke off and looked slightly puzzled.

"A toast," prompted Nancy. "A toast to what?"

Jessica wrinkled her brow. "*To the unknown.* No…it was *to the unexpected.* That was it. Then he clammed up and stared at me."

"That's not odd. You're a very attractive woman."

"A married woman," said Jessica, reaching for her coffee cup.

"Hold on!" said Nancy, pointing to Jessica's hand, poised in mid-air. "A married woman who doesn't wear a wedding ring? Since when?"

"Since…oh HELL!" Jessica hid her face in her hands. "Since last night."

"So you meet him with that huge rock on your finger, you tell everyone about your wedding anniversary, and then you show up at his place with no ring. He thought you were making a play for him."

"I'm going to throw myself off a cliff," muttered Jessica, closing her eyes.

"There aren't any cliffs on Cape Cod. C'mon, what happened next?"

"He told me a little about his life, then I started to tell him about mine. When I got to the part about getting married to Max, I was afraid I was going to start crying, so I got up and left."

"Talk about giving a man mixed signals," murmured Nancy. "The poor guy's probably down at the computer store right now, looking for an upgrade for his sexual radar."

"Don't make jokes about this, Nancy! I've made an utter fool of myself! What am I supposed to do *now*?"

Nancy shrugged. "You can start by not getting so worked up about it. So many women have been putting the moves on Rick that he'd probably have been surprised if you didn't."

"Oh, that *really* makes me feel better."

"C'mon, tell me what he said about his life! This is a small town where everyone knows everybody, and he's been awful close-mouthed about his past. The rumors going around town make him out like a combination of the reincarnation of Rudolph Valentino,

Bruce Wayne, and the Count of Monte Cristo."

"I don't think he's a French count, but there's probably something to the Caped Crusader idea." Jessica wrinkled her brow. "He didn't have time to say much. He's from somewhere in Texas…Houston, I think. He came to Cape Cod on some mission to save the planet because he thinks he helped destroy it and…"

A knock at the front door interrupted her.

"Customers, dammit," whispered Nancy. "Just when the gossip's getting good. If we're really quiet, maybe they'll go away."

"That's no way to run a business, and you know it." Jessica rose and walked to the door. "Besides, I'm ready to drop this story."

"I'm not," said Nancy plaintively.

"Jessica, darling!" cried Lois and Bill in unison. The couple who lived two doors away held a pot of African violets and a plate of brownies. "We just had to wish you luck on opening day. Ooh, look at that fabulous pewter pitcher, Bill!"

"Sorry I can't stay and chat. I was just leaving," said Nancy, picking up the box with the locket. "Nice seeing you, Lois, Bill."

Jessica walked her to the door. "Not a word about last night, please."

"Lips sealed. But only if I get the rest of the story real soon."

"I promise," whispered Jessica, squeezing Nancy's hand. She turned to Lois. "I found that pewter set at a small auction house outside Montpellier."

The rest of the day passed swiftly. After Lois and Bill left, Dan Kelly came by and bought a silver brush-and-comb set for his granddaughter's graduation. The executive committee of the Historical Society showed up as a group, and Polly Ford bought a Victorian doll's house bed for her sister Meggie's birthday.

By 6:30, Jessica had rung up over $700 in sales. An excellent first day. As she unhooked the "Open" shingle from the Wilder House sign in the drive, she noticed Rick collecting his mail. Damn. He was crossing the street.

"I need to apologize for last night," she murmured when he reached her side. "I'm not too good in stressful situations."

"Dinner with me is that stressful?"

"Of course not." Jessica hooked the "Closed" shingle beneath the sign. "Maybe it was opening day jitters."

"So how was your opening day?"

"Better than I hoped for."

"Planning to celebrate?"

"Um, not actually."

"Then let's have a drink."

"Oh, I don't want to put you to any trouble…"

"What trouble? I've got a half bottle of some pretty exquisite Bordeaux at my place. Shall we finish it off?"

"I just…"

The rest of Jessica's reply was drowned out as a black van pulled into the driveway and screeched to stop beside them.

Chapter Twenty

A thin, angular woman in a 1980s fuchsia ensemble with giant shoulder-pads hopped out of the front seat. Her black hair, highlighted with shocking pink bangs, was sprayed into spikes and splashed with frosted sequins. She pulled off a pair of oversized sunglasses and teetered toward Jessica and Rick in patent-leather stiletto sandals.

"Chris? What on earth are you doing here?" asked Jessica before realizing that introductions were in order. "Rick, this is Chris Bart, my old college roommate. Chris, this is my neighbor, Rick Martell."

"Pleased to meet you," said Rick, looking closely at the new arrival as she batted several pounds of sparkling mascara at him.

"You've trying to figure out where you've seen me before, aren't you?" she said, giving him a mega kilowatt smile. "I'm the host and executive producer of Boston Deco. Monday, Wednesday, and Friday at 9 on Channel 43."

"She doesn't usually look like this, Rick, even on television," said Jessica quickly. "Chris, whatever happened to your hair?"

"We taped a segment about 1980s memorabilia in a gonzo Roxbury hair salon where the owner channels KISS," said Chris. "Let me tell you, if these damn sequins don't wash out like he promised, I'll bounce that bozo right back to his home planet. But back to business." Chris turned to Jessica. "You honestly weren't expecting me tonight?"

"Actually… no."

"Wake up, Jessica, this is TV. You said we could tape, and this shop of yours is going to be old news next week."

"I thought antique shops were always old news," said Rick.

"You know, that's a not a bad line, Nick. I may use it tomorrow. By the way, Jessica, you wouldn't believe the fleabag motel my assistant booked for us. Do you by any chance have an extra mattress in there?"

"Uh, yes," said Jessica cautiously, peering at the van. A gray-haired man with a goatee and a younger blond man were hunched over a clipboard. "How many are you?"

"Just me. The crew is fine with fleas," said Chris quickly. "Guys, this is the antique place we're doing. We'll start at eight tomorrow, so bring a couple of gallons of skim-milk latté, Chet. Randy, could you get my suitcase from the back?"

"You got it, Chief," said Chet as he started the motor. The fresh-faced blond boy dropped a duffel bag on the front step, jogged back to the van, and jumped into the front seat. Chet tooted the horn twice and pulled into the early evening traffic.

"You two probably have a lot of catching up to do," said Rick. "Do I have a raincheck on that celebration, Jessica?"

"You're bailing already, Rock? Well, it was nice to meet you." Chris draped an arm over Jessica's shoulder and waved goodbye with the other. "Who's the hunk?"

she whispered as they walked to the door.

"He's just a neighbor." Jessica picked up the duffel and deposited it in the front hallway. "It's really great to see you."

"You too, babe." Chris looked approvingly at the antiques on display. "This'll look fantastic on cable. But first thing's first. Got anything to drink?"

Jessica led the way to the kitchen. "White wine okay?" She opened the fridge and poured two glasses of Chardonnay. "I was planning to call you in a few days to set up the interview."

"Ace reporters don't wait for phone calls, even when we're stuck on the boring home décor front," said Chris, raising her glass. "Gotta say though, tracking you took more detective skill than I expected. What the hell's going on in Boston?"

"What do you mean?"

"When you didn't answer your cell, I phoned the gallery and left a message. Nothing. Got some snotty-voiced guy at your house who told me that you were away 'indefinitely' and that Max was 'indisposed', whatever that means." Chris pulled an electronic cigarette from her purse and raised her eyebrows questioningly. Jessica nodded. "I was starting to wonder if Max had clubbed you with an antique andiron or vice versa."

"You thought one of us was *dead*?"

"Murder in a Back Bay antique emporium…" Chris said with more than a touch of regret in her voice. "You gotta admit, it would have been one hell of a scoop for Boston Deco." She took a long, satisfying swig of wine and wiped her lips. "Where was I? Oh yeah. So the next day, I showed up at the gallery and talked to this pudgy blond preppie."

"That would be Eddie," said Jessica faintly.

"Yeah, Eddie. I practically had to bribe him to get the name of your shop. I scheduled a couple of other segments in the Cape Cod area, and here I am. We'll tape you tomorrow morning bright and early and get out of your way." Chris pulled a smart phone out of her purse and slid a fuchsia fingernail over the screen. "Then we're off to Falmouth to interview some poor slob who collects scrimshaw." Chris grimaced. "Scrimshaw? That's like, sailboats carved into chunks of petrified fish or something?"

Jessica nodded. "Whalebone."

"Sounds disgusting to me." Chris sighed. "Disgusting and boring. Some people should get a life."

"Why are you doing a show like 'Boston Deco' if you hate New England collectibles so much?"

"The station head whispered 'producer' to me, and I forgot to ask what I'd be producing. By the way, I really appreciate the bed and breakfast, and it frees up my expense account. Can I take you out for a burger or something?"

"I've got a fridge full of food, so let's defrost something."

"Fine with me." Chris opened the freezer and shuffled through the boxes. "Hey, we've got the same old family recipe for lasagna. Where's the microwave?"

"Don't have one."

"You take this antique stuff way too seriously." Chris twisted the oven dial. "Now give me the real scoop. Like what you're doing down *here* and what Max is doing up *there*?"

"Chris, I really…"

"You really don't want to talk about it, right?" Chris slit open the cellophane wrapper with her fingernail and slid the lasagna into the oven. "For pete's sake, Jessica, this is a slumber party. At slumber parties, girls are supposed to *share*."

Jessica shook her head.

"At least bring me up to speed on the supporting roles. What's the dirt on that scumbag Eddie?"

"You think Eddie's a scumbag?"

"I covered politics long enough to know a scumbag when I see one. What's his story?"

Jessica shrugged helplessly.

"Puh-leeze don't pull this deaf-mute act when I'm quizzing you about your eighteenth-century toasters and Colonial computer pads tomorrow." Chris rose and stretched. "Mind if I shower and shampoo before we eat? Then I'll tell you all about my lousy love life since yours seems to be off-limits."

Chapter Twenty-One

Eddie poured himself a second cup of coffee and clicked on the remote. He liked to get up early. It gave him a jump on the competition.

"This is Chris Bart. Today our Boston Deco crew is on location in Brewster, Massachusetts where Jessica Stratton, partner in Beacon Hill's renowned Stratton Art Gallery..."

"Partner? Not so's you'd notice..." harrumphed Eddie.

"...and we're here to learn about Jessica's specialty, American Folk Art, at Wilder House Antiques, which she just opened on Cape Cod's scenic Route 6A. Tell me, Jessica, what exactly is American Folk Art?"

"There's no easy definition, Chris. For some people, it's a painting by Andrew Wyeth or Grandma Moses. I use the term to describe all the beautiful artisanal objects that most people, even the craftspeople who made them, never thought of as 'Art' with a capital 'A'. That includes bed quilts, needlepoint samplers, weathervanes, even advertising art."

Boy, this promises to be a thrill and a half, thought Eddie, yawning as he lowered the volume. Trust amateurs like Jessica to get all worked up about low-ticket items like teapots and breadboxes. Still she managed to get herself on TV, and free publicity was nothing to sneeze at. Maybe I should have cultivated that nosy Bart broad when she barged into the gallery yammering for Jessica's address.

Eddie dropped that train of thought with a cynical snort. Media exposure was the last thing he needed. He'd had a damn close call yesterday. Max spotted him in the Boston Commons with Jimbo. Jimbo was a useful contact, but he dressed like a Mafia hitman in shiny suits and flashy ties. "Chatting with your fence?" Max asked later, exploding with laughter as if he'd just said the funniest thing on earth. Of course, it *was* kind of funny. For once, poor naïve Max hit the nail on the head. Jimbo *was* a fence, and he was a damned good one.

Eddie snorted again and nearly sloshed coffee all over the crimson cashmere bathrobe he'd appropriated from Max's wardrobe. Seducing Max back in prep school had been one of the soundest investments Eddie ever made. Max's townhouse made a perfect hideout. Interpol had sniffed too close for comfort around those Klimt forgeries, and Eddie considered himself a lucky man that he'd skipped out of Prague before the situation blew up in his face. He'd taken a financial beating, though, and only managed to get a fraction of his inventory safely out of the country. Nope, a jail stint was *not* in Eddie's plans for the future.

However, Max's non-stop moping was almost enough to make prison sex sound inviting. All that moaning about *Jessica, Jessica, Jessica.* Eddie was having an increasingly hard time keeping a straight face during Max's cognac-fueled, post-orgasm soliloquies. *Am I gay? Am I not gay? Am I really gay?*

What part of "*doing it with a guy*" didn't Max

understand? Eddie sighed and buttered another piece of toast. Making out with those horse-faced debutantes after country club dances was more fun than this. As soon as he had some cash in hand, Eddie would blow this Puritan pop-stand and head for Southeast Asia, where a small bribe went a long way and where men with Eddie's omnivorous sexual appetites were easily gratified.

Eddie's eyes flickered back to the screen. The TV babe looked like she was hyperventilating over some brass andirons that would be worth more if they were melted down. Then something in the background captured all Eddie's attention: the magnificent torso of an exceptionally pretty Indian Princess wearing a complicated headdress with two broken feathers. That meant something…but what?

Eddie had a terrific memory. He could have cheated his way to *summa cum laude* back at Yale, but he didn't need to bother with crib sheets. One glance at a text and he could recite the entire book by heart. Something about those broken feathers triggered a story he'd heard long, long ago. He raised the volume.

"…*quite a spectacular conversation piece*," gushed Chris. "*Can you tell us something about it?*"

"*It's a fairly atypical example of nineteenth-century cigar store advertising, even if female figures were used far less often than men.*"

"*If restaurants still had smoking sections it might work,*" quipped Chris. "*However, it's hardly a practical collectible for a two-room city apartment, is it? Now, what about this decoy duck?*"

Eddie switched the TV off. There was something about this Indian Princess babe that smelled like money in the bank. The statue looked familiar somehow... but where, when, why? It would come to him later. And in the meantime, it was time to wake up dreary old Max and ask him a few pointed questions about his wife's Folk Art collection.

Chapter Twenty-Two

"Child, what do you think of that Revolutionary War chess set?" Mrs. Braithwaite's high-pitched nasal voice threatened to shatter the etched glass goblet that she waved absent-mindedly. Melanie, who was polishing a set of brass candlesticks in the corner, looked up in such abject terror that Jessica bit her lip to keep from laughing.

Rebecca Braithwaite was a loud, arrogant woman, convinced that she was an expert on every aspect of the antique trade. Despite the unseasonably warm spring weather, the client wore a heavy tweed jacket which, though several sizes too small, didn't hamper her considerable lung power. Mrs. Braithwaite screeched like a wounded hyena every time she asked for a price and resolutely ignored all Jessica's suggestions, preferring to bark questions at unsuspecting clients after getting their attention by rapping their shins with a silver-tipped cane that she'd appropriated shortly after entering the store.

"Um, I think the chess set is, um, very historical and pretty," stammered Melanie helplessly, looking to Jessica for approval.

Jessica braced her shoulders as if going into battle, resisting the impulse to snatch the glass goblet from Mrs. Braithwaite's sweaty fingers and return it to safety on the shelf. She picked up the "King" chess piece of the American army, modeled after George Washington, and one of the British pawns. "The workmanship is excellent. Look at the attention to detail. Every musket is different, every uniform button is gilded."

Mrs. Braithwaite stared at Jessica disapprovingly then turned back to Melanie. "Well, child, I admit that it's a pretty plaything. But $750 is a lot of money. It's *shockingly* overpriced."

"$850," said Jessica firmly.

"Shockingly overpriced," repeated Mrs. Braithwaite.

Jessica sighed. It was a big sale, but it wasn't worth lowering the price any farther from the $975 that the chess set had been originally ticketed. Since Chris's broadcast last week, the shop had been filled with eager customers. If Jessica didn't have ten years of collected merchandise in reserve, she'd have had to plan a buying trip.

"We both know she can do better than $850, my dear child," continued Mrs. Braithwaite, changing tactics and addressing Melanie in a cloying, honey-coated tone. "I saw the very same chess set in New Orleans last year, and it was only $300."

Jessica winked at Melanie over Mrs. Braithwaite's shoulder. Since school was out, Melanie had been able to work at Wilder House on a regular schedule. Jessica looked across the street, where the windows of the gray-shingled cottage were tightly shuttered. Rick Martell had been called out of town before he'd been able to make good on that raincheck for a dinner date.

That was probably for the best. He was attractive as hell, but being with him meant making a decision on how to come to terms with the Max-and-Jessica question, not to mention the Max-and-Eddie question. Throwing herself into work and avoiding all thoughts of Rick Martell seemed like the best solution.

So why did she keep staring at his house, hoping to see his jeep in the driveway?

"I'll take it," said Mrs. Braithwaite suddenly. She snapped open a thick burgundy wallet.

"Hmm?" Jessica looked up in surprise.

"I still say it's robbery." Mrs. Braithwaite counted out nine crisp $100 bills and laid them on the cherry wood desk. She glared angrily at the $50 change. Jessica smothered a triumphant grin as she wrote out a receipt on embossed Wilder House notepaper.

Mrs. Braithwaite stuffed the receipt in her purse after scrutinizing it suspiciously and stalked to the door, leaning heavily on the antique cane. "And I want that chess set gift wrapped. I'll come back for it after lunch."

"Excuse me, did you also want to purchase that cane?" asked Jessica politely.

"No, I do *not* want to purchase this cane." Mrs. Braithwaite dumped it unceremoniously in the umbrella stand at the entrance. "And about that gift wrap, I want every single piece wrapped separately." She turned on her heels, beckoned imperiously to her driver, and let the screen door slam behind her.

"What a disgusting old cow!" said Melanie indignantly as the car drove off. "There's gotta be a million pieces in a chess set!"

"Thirty-two, plus the board," said Jessica absently as she tallied the sale in the daily ledger. "We made the sale, but she's taking revenge on our ribbon supply."

"Thirty-two?" exclaimed Melanie in dismay. "It's

gonna take me forever." She picked up the chessboard and carried it into the kitchen where Jessica had set up an impromptu wrapping desk. Nancy had been right as rain about that. No one had ever asked for gift-wrapping at Stratton Gallery, but nearly every Wilder House client insisted on it.

What a way to make a living, Jessica thought as she slid Mrs. Braithwaite's $850 into the plastic pouch she'd deposit at the Cape Cod Savings Bank later this afternoon. Clients who approached every purchase like a prizefight depressed her. Max had treated people like Mrs. Braithwaite with such chilling contempt that they were grateful to get out of the gallery alive. His squint reduced both amateur and experienced bargainers to jelly. Jessica picked up a small pewter mirror and practiced squinting.

No, that wasn't any good. She looked like a badger with a migraine. How about a professional sneer? She narrowed her eyes, curled her lip, and stared at her reflection with such snide concentration that she didn't hear the knocking on the door. When the sound finally registered, she had to stifle the impulse to shout "Go away". It was probably Mrs. Braithwaite, refreshed and ready for another round.

"Jessica, can't you hear that? Someone's knocking real loud." Melanie walked out of the kitchen, a strand of gold ribbon trailing in her wake.

When Jessica didn't answer, Melanie peeked through the front window and squealed in delight. "It's Mr. Martell!" She threw open the door. "You're back! How was Nova Scotia?"

"Dirty and slimy." Rick dropped a nylon overnight case on the floor and looked at Jessica, who was trying to recompose her features into a welcoming smile after her sneering practice.

"You were in Canada?" she asked.

"He was checking out this oil slick," bubbled Melanie. "For a research project, right? On environmental impact, right? Did you just get back?"

"Yes, and I was on my way to see you."

"Me?" Melanie flushed, suddenly speechless.

"I ran into your mother at the airport. She was waiting for a client..."

"Mr. Conover," interjected Melanie. "He's got a hedge fund. He's got this really cool private plane."

"His really cool private plane is grounded in Nantucket for the moment. Your mother wanted to let you know that she couldn't meet you for lunch."

"Is that all?" asked Melanie, barely hiding her disappointment.

"I think that was it," said Rick with a little smile.

"Oh," said Melanie, looking down at her shoes and fingering her forget-me-not locket.

"What a pretty necklace," said Rick kindly.

Melanie looked up, her face aglow with happiness. "My mother gave it to me for my sixteenth birthday."

"And all the gold streamers?"

Melanie looked down again. She was trailing ten feet of satin ribbon from the wrapping desk. "Darn it. That old bat will be coming back for her stupid chess set. Gotta get back to work."

"Atta girl," Jessica said.

Melanie pirouetted and sashayed back to the kitchen, taking most of the animation with her. Rick sank wearily into the sofa and rubbed his shoulder gently.

"Rick? Are you feeling all right?"

"It's just exhaustion." He flashed a reassuring smile, but it looked like it cost an effort. "Six hours in a plane that was designed for dwarfs. Then the cartons with all the water samples got mislaid. I've spent the last few hours at the airport while they tried to track them down."

He shrugged ruefully, stretching his long legs. "But that wasn't the worst part. Miles and miles of polluted beachfront. And why?" His eyes flashed. "Because broken-down oil tankers are floating around the world like ecological timebombs."

In the kitchen, Melanie pushed her chair closer to the door, which she'd left slightly ajar. Scissors and ribbon in hand, she leaned toward the opening.

"…working too hard and too long," Jessica was saying. "You need some rest."

"What I need is a few hours on a healthy beach." Rick leaned over and grasped both of Jessica's hands. "Lock this place up, and we'll go to the National Seashore. We can sit by the dunes, listen to the gulls…"

Melanie nearly clapped her hands with delight. A totally grown-up afternoon at the beach with Rick and Jessica. A private nature class too, she bet. Kim Adams would be green with envy when she found out.

"Rick, I can't abandon the store."

"You're the boss, aren't you?" asked Rick, not letting go of her hands. "Have you been to the beach *once* since you moved here?"

Jessica shook her head.

"Jessica, that's a crime, but you can make up for it by saying yes. Melanie can run the shop, can't she?"

The plastic tape dispenser Melanie was holding

slipped from her fingers and skidded across the tile floor. *He expects me to stay here while he takes Jessica to the beach? Could he be interested in her? Doesn't he know she's married? It's wrong, and it's totes unfair. Unfair. Unfair. Unfair!*

"She's only sixteen, Rick. I can't leave her all alone."

"So close up for a few hours. Who's going to go shopping on a gorgeous sunny day like today?"

"Nobody in their right mind," Jessica admitted. She looked out the window at the bright golden sun and the cloudless sapphire sky. "Nobody but Mrs. Braithwaite."

"Forget about her, whoever she is."

"She's unforgettable, and she's coming back to pick up the chess set that Melanie is wrapping. If the shop's closed when she gets here, she'll report me to the Better Business Bureau."

In the kitchen, Melanie twirled a curl of satin ribbon between her thumb and forefinger resentfully. Everyone took her for a dumb kid. Like that stupid old hag this morning who kept calling her "Child" every few minutes. *Child?* Sixteen was old enough to get married and have a child of her own in a whole lot of states. She'd play it cool though. Just like Mom did, hiding her disappointment when a client changed his mind a few days before a sale went through. Besides, it was just a matter of time until Jessica went back to her husband.

"I heard you say something about going to the beach." Melanie walked into the front room, head high, hoping that her voice sounded devastatingly mature. "I can wait for Mrs. Braithwaite and close the store."

"I'm not sure, Melanie…" began Jessica.

But Rick had already bounded across the room. "You're a princess, kiddo!" He threw his arms around Melanie and lifted her off her feet. Despite the fact that he'd called her "kiddo" and forgotten to include her on the beach trip, Melanie nearly swooned with pleasure.

"Jessica, I'll drop off my bag and be back in fifteen minutes. Will you be ready?"

"Sure, but I have to stop at the bank on the way to deposit the day's receipts."

"No problem." Rick blew another kiss to Melanie, picked up his suitcase, and headed out the door.

"There's food in the kitchen if you're hungry. Do you remember how to set the security alarm?" asked Jessica as she headed up the stairs.

Melanie followed her. "Yep, the place where I babysat last summer had the same system. Piece of cake."

"And the code?" Jessica rooted through her bureau drawers for something to wear. Her swimsuit was still in Boston, so cut-offs and a T-shirt would have to do.

"0946Z. You're awfully pale. You better borrow my sunscreen." Melanie had some even more crucial advice, but she wasn't sure how to present it. Jessica, smart as she was about old plates and posters and stuff, didn't have a clue about how things worked in a small town. A married woman stepping out with the hottest guy in town? You might as well call CNN.

By the time Jessica had tossed a towel in her bag, Rick was out front, pulling down the canvas top of his jeep. Jessica hesitated on the front step.

"Ready to go?" he asked.

"Just a minute." Jessica turned to Melanie. "Remember, don't let anyone in except Mrs.

Braithwaite."

"Nobody gets in but the old cow."

"And lock up right after."

"Right after the cow goes home."

Jessica got into the jeep and fastened the seatbelt. Melanie pushed the car door shut. She'd fluffed her opportunity to say anything important to Jessica, and what was worse, it was downright *pitiful* to see Rick looking so happy. Like he thought this was a *date* or something.

"Take care of Lady Hiawatha," said Jessica.

Lady Hiawatha? What nonsense was she talking about now? "We'll all be just fine," said Melanie firmly. She waved as the jeep pulled into the road and walked back to the house.

The wrapping project was almost finished. Just three pawns, two bishops, and one more knight to go. Melanie cut six tiny squares of Jessica's flowery Victorian gift paper, rolled each piece in fresh tissue, taped and tied a ribbon around each.

Now what? If Mrs. Blimp took as long to eat her lunch as she did to buy a chess set, Melanie could be stuck here all day. She was afraid to put on her headphones too. What if Mrs. B rang on the landline and she missed it? Resentfully, Melanie popped a can of soda and ripped open a box of chocolate chip cookies.

She was stretched out on the sofa, flipping through one of Jessica's totally boring art magazines, when she heard a knock at the door. A blond, good-looking man…well, maybe a little too fat to be totally swoon-worthy…in a rumpled beige suit.

Melanie hastily swallowed the rest of her cookie

and rose to her feet. "I'm sorry, we're closed for the day."

"I'm not a *client*, my dear," said Eddie, lowering his eyes meekly, a trick with a hundred percent success rate that he'd perfected after observing cocker spaniels beg for treats. "I'm Max Stratton, Jessica's husband. And I really, really need your help."

Chapter Twenty-Three

The bank teller at Cape Cod Five was taking his own sweet time filling out the deposit slip. Jessica looked out the plate-glass window and waved helplessly to Rick, outside in the car, who was making phone calls. He waved back, then reached into the glove compartment for a well-worn regional map.

"Thanks, Mark. See you back at the lab."

Rick hung up, grinning with satisfaction. Jessica had mentioned a fondness for secluded beaches when they were discussing the Cape's varied waterfront options. There were tame, marshy beaches on the bay; tranquil stretches of sand on the scenic Nantucket Sound; and the wilder, Atlantic surf beaches. *Secluded*, however, was not a slam-dunk on any of the above. At least, not on a sunny afternoon after Memorial Day.

But Rick had managed it.

Mark Depman, one of the Boston-based biologists at the institute, had a beach house near Truro. And he'd given everyone at the lab an open invitation to use his private beach whenever they wanted.

Rick couldn't even imagine Martine wanting a secluded beach. The only beach he'd seen with her was part of a five-star hotel complex on the French Riviera. According to Martine, the whole point of the "seaside experience" was pecking at a three-course lunch at the hotel's gourmet restaurant with an audience who could appreciate her bejeweled sandals, designer sunglasses, and an itsy-bitsy bikini that cost about $75 per square inch.

Private Cape Cod beach…check. Gourmet lunch? Rick glanced at the basket of fancy sandwiches, iced tea, cookies, and apples he'd bought at the designer deli across the street from the bank. Check.

With a few quiet hours and no distractions, he just might be able to figure out what was going on with his mysterious neighbor. This time there would be no well-meaning real estate agents to run interference. No ancient mariners with post-hole diggers. No college roommates with television crews. And hopefully, no damn cigar-store Indians.

Dessert? Should he get some dessert? There was a teenage boy on the corner selling cookies from cart with a bright red canopy. Martine wouldn't have eaten a calorie-packed cookie to save her life, but who knows? Jessica might like one. After some consideration, Rick chose a health-conscious peach granola square and (on the boy's advice) a sinfully decadent triple-chocolate brownie.

All dessert bases covered. He noticed the boy's attention was wandering as he handed him the money and looked over his shoulder. Yep, there was Jessica striding across the street in those faded cut-offs and her vintage Velvet Underground T-shirt. She waved at Rick, he waved back, and Rick acknowledged the heartfelt envy and respect with which the kid returned his change. "Thanks," he said. "We'll enjoy the cookies."

"Sorry for the delay," said Jessica when she joined him at the car. "There was a problem with my mailing address."

"Big problem?" asked Rick as he eased into traffic.

"My new company checkbook was sent to the Centerville branch."

"Well, that's closer than Central Asia, which is probably where my water samples are by now. If Fate's giving us an overdue vacation, let's be grateful."

Because, Rick added to himself, if those cartons *hadn't* gone missing, he wouldn't be taking another chance on Jessica, a woman with more baggage than Hercules could handle with a forklift. The first time they met, she'd tried to smash his head in. Then she added insult to injury with that politically incorrect Indian image. And—in an act of sheer blasphemy for any Texan—she barely touched his signature three-alarm *chili con carne* before going AWOL on him.

Jessica Stratton was a puzzle and a half, all right. He snuck a glance at her as they drove through the town. When she was silent, she radiated waves of sadness. Rick had learned enough about loneliness since he'd sworn off female company post-Martine to recognize the symptoms in a fellow sufferer. What Jessica Stratton needed now was a friend, and the inconvenient thing about friendship was that he was getting more attracted to her all the time. It was easy enough to put the kibosh on any daydreams about her when she was wearing the wedding ring, but—he glanced at her hands, folded demurely on her lap—she wasn't wearing it anymore. Did he need to censor his daydreams now? Daydreams about waking up with Jessica in his king-size bed the morning after all the glorious things they'd done in the bed the night before?

Wedding rings or not, he'd done his best to "X" her

out of those X-rated visions while on assignment in Nova Scotia. After all, the woman had big relationship conflicts, and she'd run away from his home-cooked dinner as if he'd been serving her poison pigeon fritters. *Yes*, she'd be hard to ignore, as she lived right across the street. *Yes,* any sane man would label Jessica Stratton as "must avoid."

…and here he was…

…wondering if sanity was overrated.

A few hours ago, in the airport café, he'd been swearing under his breath as he filled out claim forms dreamed up by a Siberian sadist when he heard a friendly, familiar voice. Nancy Webster slid into the booth and motioned to the waitress for more coffee. "Lost your luggage?" she asked, glancing at his paperwork. "My client's grounded in Nantucket 'indefinitely.' Can we talk about *anything* but airport hassles?"

"Jessica*,*" Rick heard himself say before he could stop himself. "Please tell me about Jessica."

****

"What a blissful escape," said Jessica. They were stretched out on Rick's plaid beach blanket, their own private island in the sand. The dunes behind them sparkled with beach plum blossoms, and bright blue waves crested in a lacy foam that lapped along the shoreline. Opportunistic seagulls, having made short work of the bread crusts, had flown off again, leaving them on their own.

"Escape from what?" Rick was still trying to fathom what Nancy had said, and *not* said, this morning. Clearly, Nancy ranked Jessica's husband as a negative 5 on a scale of 1 to 10, while hinting that, sooner or later, Jessica was bound to notice that Rick Martell was a solid 12.

"Escape from everything." Jessica uncapped the sunblock that Melanie had thrust on her and started again. "Rick, you probably think I'm a little bit crazy…"

"Agreed."

"What's that supposed to mean?" Jessica looked up indignantly as she rubbed the lotion into her arms.

"The lady who smells like a fruit salad wants clarification on that?"

Jessica glanced at the neon yellow tube of sunscreen gel that Melanie had pressed on her. "Supersonic Papaya Parfait, SPF 30," she read out loud. "You're right, I do smell like fruit salad. But Rick, there's something I haven't told you, and it's important. I'm married."

"Yes."

"The problem is that I'm not really *sure* that I'm married. Not anymore. I *ought* to be sure, but I'm not." Jessica stared out at the waves. "Does any of that make sense?"

"Not really."

"You see…" Jessica took a deep breath. "When I got back to Boston, the night of my anniversary, I found my husband in bed with his old business partner." She flushed. "I used to think I had the perfect life and the perfect marriage and since this hit me, I'm not sure of anything anymore."

"Ah," said Rick. Nancy hadn't furnished any specific details. So that's why she'd done a very convincing imitation of a fire-breathing dragon when she mentioned Jessica's husband. "That's rough. This, um…this ex-business associate of your husband's…she wasn't a girlfriend of yours, was she?"

"Not a friend. Not a girl."

"Come again?"

"My husband's cheating on me with a man, Rick. He's gay…or bisexual…I don't know. He's been having an affair with a man he's known for more than thirty years. And since my husband's very prominent in Boston society, I was probably the last person in Massachusetts to know."

"Oh, Jessica." Rick put his arms around her shoulders and squeezed.

The he started laughing.

Low at first. Then louder and louder.

"WHAT is so funny about this?" asked Jessica angrily, squirming away from him. "My husband cheats on me with some creep from his prep school tennis team, and you think it's all a giant joke?"

"Not at all, Jessica. Not at all." Rick got a bottle of mineral water from the picnic basket and offered it to Jessica, who shook her head. He took a deep swig and re-capped it. "Why don't I tell you about *my* late, great love affair. Martine Dulac.

"Was she French?" asked Jessica.

"Oh yes, and she hit on me like I was the last chunk of *foie gras* on earth. I was doing research on an oil rig off the Texas coast. She was photographing it for a magazine. Two years we were together, except for the weeks when she was overseas 'on assignment', and I never suspected…"

"Suspected what?"

"That she was married. In fact, she was married to an oil lobbyist based in London. Turns out, he'd *asked* her to cozy up with an engineer on the pipeline project and push me toward corporate HQ. After I got the PR job, she fed him everything she learned from me."

"And when you found out, you broke up with her?"

"Are you kidding?" Rick picked up a clam shell and tossed it toward the surf. "Martine dumped *me* as soon as I quit Big Oil. She had no use for a born-again ecologist. Or perhaps I should say that Martine's *husband* had no more use for me. So when it comes to betrayal and being the last to know about a partner's intentions, you and I, we've got a tie score. The question is, where do we go from here?"

"Like, in a year from now?"

"I was thinking about tonight. We've got a raincheck on drinks, and I've still got a lot of leftover chili. You know, wine isn't the only thing that improves with age. Those chili peppers are fermenting up a whole Texas firestorm of flavor."

"I'm thinking more like a walk down the beach," said Jessica. "And who knows? Since we've both been so unlucky in love…"

"…we should start a poker game?" asked Rick.

"No, I was thinking that we might find a buried treasure."

"Is it always about treasure with you?" asked Rick, helping her to her feet.

"Treasure's everywhere, Rick. Yesterday, a single mom came to the shop with an old weathervane she'd found in her grandmother's closet. She was ready to paint it yellow and use it as a nursery mobile, but it was a rare nineteenth-century piece that could fetch as much as $4,000 at auction. She was thrilled when I told her. It will be enough to pay all her hospital bills."

"I thought the whole point was giving her twenty bucks for it and selling it for yourself for a huge mark-up."

"If I'd bought that weathervane for twenty dollars at an auction, it would have been my treasure and I'd have done just that. But this time, it was someone else's treasure."

"So I guess the weathervane story had a happy ending," said Rick. He stooped to extract a small beige tube from a clump of seaweed. "And here's our first treasure of the day."

"What on earth is it?" asked Jessica as she turned the fragile object over in her hands. Several dry, parchment-like compartments were held together by a darker string-like coil. "Is it animal, vegetable, or mineral?"

"It's a whelk egg-case," answered Rick. "Hold out your hands."

He cracked open one of the compartments and minute, perfectly formed spiral shells spilled into her palm.

"Marvelous," said Jessica in awe. "They're like dollhouse shells."

"The beach is filled with treasures. You never know what you'll find."

"But if these are baby whelks, don't they need to be in the ocean to survive?"

"Honestly, I don't know much about neo-natal mollusks, but I think these are long dead."

"But maybe they aren't! Maybe we can save them. Like the Titanic in reverse," said Jessica. She ran to the water's edge and waded in.

"Hey! Watch out, Jessica! Mark says there's a

wicked undertow." Rick followed, after pausing briefly to roll up the legs of his chinos.

"What did you say?"

Rick waded up to her. "Undertow. Water moving away from the shore. Watch your step."

"I don't feel anything." Jessica walked a few feet farther, until the waves lapped her knees. Winding her arm like a baseball pitcher, she threw the egg-case as far as she could. "Ooooh," she shrieked as the water swirled around her ankles and she lost her balance.

Rick was at her side in a second. "Gotcha," he said as he lifted her high above the waves, his lips brushing her cheek. "When waves break on the shore and return the sea, they gain enough momentum to sweep you off your feet, which is why it's called undertow. WHOA!" he shouted as the tide grabbed his ankles and pulled him down.

They were shaking with cold as they crawled out of the frigid water and sat by the water's edge.

"That," said Rick as he unbuttoned his soaked cotton shirt and made an attempt to wring the water out, "is an undertow with a sneaky sense of timing. Hopefully, I'll find a less slapstick way to demonstrate the dynamics of undertow to the summer school kids."

"I don't know. Practical demonstrations sure get the point across quickly," said Jessica wryly. She cast a sidelong glance at Rick. With the saltwater glistening against his bronzed torso, he looked like the statue of a Greek warrior god. "I was starting to panic when my head went under. I don't know what would have happened without you." Jessica, trembling, leaned against Rick's broad bare shoulders. "How did you stay so calm?"

"Oceanography 101. When you get swept away like that..." His eyes met Jessica's. "If you start to get swept away like that, the most important thing to remember..." His breath was a warm breeze against her cheek. "...is not to resist."

"Not to resist," repeated Jessica through chattering teeth.

"Because, eventually, the tides will...hell, you're freezing. Let's go up to the house and dry off. Mark told me where he hides the spare key."

Her flimsy T-shirt clung to the curves of her body. She looked like one of those statues of Greek goddesses, but living and breathing and, in this case, shivering. Rick's fingers ached to trace the soft curves of her shoulders, her breasts, her waist. And she hadn't actually ruled out the idea of dinner, had she? Things were looking up...

In a few minutes, they were in the house. Rick busied himself with the coffee machine, and Jessica repaired to the bathroom, where she found a hairdryer and managed to dry her underwear in a few minutes. She slipped into her long jeans and buttoned up her jeans jacket, thankful that Melanie had insisted that she pack cover-ups.

The kitchen was a sparsely decorated, masculine room with pine floors and walls. Huge picture windows overlooked the dunes, and the tantalizing aroma of hot coffee wafted through the room. Two large earthenware mugs were placed in front of the coffee pot. She poured two cups and brought them to the breakfast table where Rick, clad in a pair of gray sweatpants that she vaguely remembered seeing crumpled up in the back seat of the jeep, was scribbling notes as he talked on the phone. He hung up just as Jessica put the coffee in front of him.

"Good news?" she asked hopefully.

"Good and bad." He sipped the coffee gratefully. "Boy, that tastes good. The airline thinks they located all my cartons, but they got mixed up with a shipment of census records that was forwarded to Ottawa. If I want to claim my data without any more delays, I've got to fly up tonight before the samples get locked up in some giant warehouse outside town. The good news is that I'm booked on the 7 p.m. flight from Hyannis."

"And the bad news?"

"The bad news is that I need a raincheck on my raincheck. The lab needs to get cracking on that data right away. I'm relieved that it's been found but pissed that it's messed up our plans."

"I understand," said Jessica softly. On impulse, she put her hand on his shoulder. He turned his head, brushed his lips against her fingertips, and rose, glancing at his watch.

"If this thing's as waterproof as it's supposed to be, we've got to burn rubber to get you back home and get me to the airport."

Chapter Twenty-Four

Eddie had parked the rental car three doors down from Wilder House and had been cooling his heels, slumped low in the front seat, watching clients come and go for about an hour. He needed to examine that statue up close, but he hadn't decided on his plan of attack yet. Eddie always played these things by ear. Sooner or later, he'd sense an opening and move quickly, smoothly, and instinctively.

Opportunity knocked sooner than he expected. Jessica Stratton, carrying a big straw beach bag, hopped into a jeep driven by a sexy dude with a ponytail. They chatted for a few minutes with a teenage girl, then zoomed off. The kid looked a bit deflated as she walked back to the shop.

Jessica's got a beach boy, thought Eddie snidely. Wouldn't it be fun to twist that information into a jeweled dagger and plunge it into Max's achy breaky heart? Nah, he'd wait until there was an opportunity to profit from that info…which might not even be a profitable scoop. With a goody-goody like Jessica, her Chippendale escort was likely to be some bozo who collected seventeenth-century surfboards.

No, there was no need to rock the boat in Boston…at least not yet. The Stratton townhouse was a damned luxurious place to lie low until the next business opportunity presented itself. Max was eating out of his hand, if dipping rather heavily into the crystal decanters of single malt whisky that Eddie kept thoughtfully refilling and scattering around the townhouse.

The day job, however, was turning out to be a total drag. Eddie was doing almost all the work at the gallery, the lion's share of the paperwork on the Lenox estate sale, plus chauffeuring Max back and forth to the Berkshires to parley with the Lenox heirs since Eddie didn't care to risk his own precious life in that crazy English import hot-rod when Max had a half-bottle of whisky under his belt.

Eddie rang the bell of Wilder House. He still wasn't one-hundred percent sure how he'd play this yet. The best pitches, he'd found, rose to his lips when he came face-to-face with his prey. If you listened carefully, people would tell you just how much rope you needed to hang them and offer to tie the noose as well. The teenager answered the door, which probably meant she was alone. Perfect. Cute kid...but she was definitely down-in-the-mouth. Cooped up inside on a sunny day?

"Sorry, but the shop is closed for the day," she said flatly.

What was it? A broken heart? Puppy love for Mister Ponytail? Or just general adolescent angst?

"But I'm not a client," he said, peering through the screen and trying to get a quick read on the sullen expression in the girl's eyes. "I'm Max Stratton, Jessica's husband. And I'd like to have a little talk with you. You see, I'm very, very worried about my wife."

The door opened at once. *I should go to Hollywood and steal myself an Oscar,* thought Eddie.

"Mr. Stratton, please come in. We weren't, I mean, I don't think Jessica was expecting you." Nervously, Melanie wiped cookie crumbs from her lips with a backhand motion. "I'm sorry, but she's not here right now. It's nice to meet you though. I'm Melanie. Melanie Webster."

"Melanie Webster!" Eddie echoed heartily. The name was obviously supposed to mean something to him.

"You know. Nancy's daughter."

"Not Nancy's daughter!" *Two ways to play this.* Eddie reached over to tousle the girl's hair, and she backed away. Wrong move, but now he had his playbook. "Not Nancy's *daughter!*" he repeated in a tone of disbelief. "Why, how could I have guessed? You're not a child anymore. You're a beautiful, grown-up woman!"

Bingo. The kid lit up like a Christmas tree.

"Um, as I said, Jessica's gone out, and I'm not sure when she'll be back."

"I don't think that really matters. I'm not sure if she wants to see me right now." Eddie lowered his eyes again and tried to look as pathetic as possible. "Would you mind if we sat down inside and talked for a few minutes?"

Without waiting for an answer, he stepped over the threshold and guided Melanie into the front room. That would be where the statue was. Yes indeed. He took a seat on the couch. Now it was just a matter of getting the kid out of the room for a few minutes.

"What do you want to talk about, Mr. Stratton?"

"Please call me Max."

"Max," said Melanie.

"I guess you've noticed that I haven't been around here much."

Melanie nodded.

"I don't suppose that Jessica's told you anything about our…our separation, has she?"

"No."

Eddie sighed. "Then everything I tell you must be strictly confidential. You mustn't tell *anyone*. Will you *promise*, Melanie? I hope so, because I love my wife dearly, and I'd do anything to get her back. But for that, I'm going to need your help. Can I really trust you? Can I really, really trust you?"

"Of course," breathed Melanie.

"This is a very painful question, and I hope you'll be honest with me. Is there another man in Jessica's life? Please don't be afraid of hurting me. Tell me the truth."

Melanie fidgeted with her locket. This was terrible. What could she say? It wasn't like she really *knew* that Rick…that Rick and Jessica…

"I see," said Eddie sadly. "You suspect that there's something going on, but you aren't really sure."

"Oh, Mr. Stratton! I mean, Max. Jessica wouldn't ever do anything wrong. Jessica is…why, Jessica is…"

"…absolutely marvelous," finished Eddie. "It's not surprising that other men have noticed that as well. If only there was something that I—*and only I*—could do for her." Eddie let his voice trail away as his eyes roamed across the room and landed on the Indian statue. "Oh my goodness, does she still have *that* old monstrosity? What's she trying to sell it for?"

Melanie picked up a Wilder House price list. "It's marked NFS. That means it's not for sale."

"Dear, sweet, sentimental Jessica," said Eddie with a rueful smile. "How she loves her Lady Hiawatha."

"Lady Hiawatha?" Okay, *now* Jessica's last comment made sense. "That's exactly what she calls it!"

"It was our little nickname," confided Eddie. Dammit, that little nickname was the *only* thing he'd been able to drag out of Max this morning. Except for the fact that the statue came from Briarcrest. *Briarcrest!* The very name sent chills up Eddie's spine. Possibly the poshest nineteenth-century mansion in America. Burned to a crisp under such deliciously mysterious circumstances.

"Like a little private joke between the two of you?" asked Melanie innocently.

"I guess so, Melanie. But I never really took Jessica's fondness for this beat-up old chunk of wood seriously. Two of the feathers in the headdress are broken, and half of the arrows in her quiver are gone." Eddie crouched near the statue's base. "And just look at those scorch marks!"

Melanie got up and came closer. Eddie pointed to a rough, charred section of the otherwise smoothly burnished wood. "Can you see where the skirt has been burned?"

Melanie nodded.

"Jessica always wanted to have the statue professionally restored, but I told her it would be a scandalous waste of money." Eddie sighed. "I wonder if…"

"If what, Max?"

"Perhaps, if I got it restored now…" Eddie ran his hands over the base of the statue. "If I got it restored now, Jessica might see it as a gesture of reconciliation. If her Lady Hiawatha was all shining and beautiful one day, she'd know how much I love her. Don't you think so, Melanie?"

"I think that's super-romantic," said Melanie. "But how exactly would you go about doing that? You'd have to—"

Her query was cut short by a furious rapping on the door.

"Let me in! I haven't got all day!" The screen door did nothing to muffle Mrs. Braithwaite's strident voice.

"One moment," said Melanie politely as she unlatched the door she'd locked after letting Eddie in. "The chess set is all wrapped. If you'll wait right here, I'll go in the back and get it."

"I'm coming with you," announced Mrs. Braithwaite. "I want to make sure that every single piece is accounted for."

Melanie looked over to Eddie. "I'm sorry, Mr. Stratton. I mean, Max. This will only take a minute."

"Oh, don't worry about me," said Eddie. He bowed elegantly to both ladies and stood still until he heard the faint rustling of paper from the next room and Mrs. Braithwaite's stentorian voice slowly counting "One…two…three…"

Then he quickly turned his attention to the statue. If only this stupid lump of firewood could talk. Eddie had his own ideas about the Briarcrest blaze, a story that had fascinated him ever since he was a boy. An ultra-rich hermit living in a remote castle. A fire that destroyed everything on the Fourth of July. The bulk of the staff, enjoying the parades and concerts in town, too far away until too late to help dowse the flames.

153

All that fabulous wealth, gone in a minute. *Or had it all gone?* The way Eddie saw it, a lot of money wasn't accounted for.

The estate sale that Stratton Gallery was handling in Lenox was barely fifty miles from the ruins of Briarcrest, so Eddie did some sightseeing yesterday. There wasn't much left. Crumbling stone walls, splotched with lichen and moss. Two roofless Gothic turrets reaching out of the ground like broken limbs. A Florentine-style garden fountain that was covered with green algae and bird droppings.

Much of the mansion was wood-frame, but given the stone foundations and an unusually rainy summer, the blaze had started slowly enough for the eighty-year-old recluse and his trusty caretaker to salvage quite a lot. The domestic staff was celebrating the Fourth of July with fireworks and a dance in the nearby town, and only the caretaker stayed behind. The caretaker, who happened to be some hillbilly relation of Jessica's, helped his dying, decrepit master carry as much of the loot as possible to safety. Apparently, they'd tossed a lot of the smaller items out of the windows when the flames got fierce.

Under the pretext of research for the Lenox estate sale, Eddie had logged a good deal of time in the local library, pouring over sepia illustrations of Briarcrest in its prime. Sure enough, he spotted the Indian Princess in two pictures of the mansion's smoking room. All the feathers were intact at that time, as was the ornate bow and arrow slung over her shoulder, but it was sure enough the same sweet-faced gal.

According to the blueprints Eddie dug up, the smoking room was on the *second* floor. And that's what didn't make sense. The vogue for vintage advertising art was a relatively recent phenom. But back in the day? When Briarcrest was at its prime, a statue like that would barely qualify as decorative kitsch. What made a banal item like that worth risking life and limb to save?

Eddie wrapped his arms around the statue's waist and tried to lift it. It felt a little too light for solid wood, but it was still cumbersome as hell. Eddie estimated that it would take several experienced movers to get this hulk down the mansion's marble staircase intact. And with just two men? One of them elderly? Both of them choking in the smoke? Forget it…it was no wonder that most of the statue's delicate appendages got snapped off in transit.

Contemporary insurance investigators figured that the old hermit hid his sizeable fortune under the mattress and that it had been burned up since the bank accounts were almost empty. Stories where large amounts of cold hard cash disappeared into thin air were NOT the kind of stories that Eddie liked…not unless Eddie had played a prominent role in the said disappearance.

Eddie ran his hands over the statue again. If his theory was correct, there was a hidden panel somewhere. But his fingers felt no joint, and his tiny penlight revealed no hairline cracks. He wished there was enough space in the crowded shop to tip the statue over and examine the underside of the base. He crawled under a display case and stretched his fingers as far underneath as he could.

AHA! A piece of wood veneer was nailed to the bottom of the stand. A little prying with his trusty Swiss army knife paid off. The ancient nails gave up and, after thrusting the thin piece of wood under the sofa, Eddie's index finger located a tiny indentation that felt like a keyhole. Yes! If only someone else hadn't got to it first. Eddie's blood ran icy cold for a minute. But no…no way. According to Max, Jessica's family were practically paupers. In a rare rush of emotion, Eddie put his lips to the statue's feet and kissed her wooden boots. "Come to daddy, baby," he whispered.

"And you tell that boss of yours that she's a dyed-in-the-wool thief! $850! That's sheer robbery!" a voice from the backroom proclaimed indignantly.

Eddie stifled a laugh. What did any of these fools know about robbery?

"I do hope your nephew will enjoy the chess set," said Melanie, following Mrs. Braithwaite to the door. "Why, where did he go?" She looked around in confusion. "Mr. Stratton? Max? Where are you?"

"Right here, dear," said Eddie, rising awkwardly from the floor and dusting the knees of his poplin suit. "I was just inspecting the fire damage around the base of the statue."

"Smart man," harrumphed Mrs. Braithwaite. "Dealers have no scruples. They'll sell you any kind of trash and pretend it came from the Czar's palace." She swept out, letting the screen door clatter noisily in her wake.

"Tough customer?" asked Eddie.

"The absolute WORST!" said Melanie emphatically. "I don't see how Jessica puts up with creeps like that. So what do you think about the statue? Can you fix it up?"

"I think so, but it can't be done here. I need to get it out of the store for a few hours." Eddie thought quickly.

He itched to take the statue right now, but he'd need a truck, and Jessica might be back any minute. Besides, he might not have to move it. He could come down with a set of lock picks, courtesy of his good pal Jimbo, and take it from there. Of course, if the lock was jammed…or the kid refused to split while he worked…well, he'd have a truck just in case.

"But how could you move it without Jessica knowing? She's always here and, when she isn't, the place is all locked up."

"That," said Eddie, "is why I need your help. We'll do it on a day when you're manning the fort."

"But today isn't a normal day. I mean, she never leaves me alone here. I was just waiting for that one client, and then I'm closing up. I usually don't even have the keys."

"But you're a smart girl," said Eddie persuasively. "You can figure something out. You see, the sooner that Jessica and I are back together where we belong, everything will be for the best."

Melanie's eyelashes flickered in agreement. Jessica and Rick together was certainly NOT for the best. She'd looked up Rick's rental lease in her mom's file cabinet yesterday. Rick's birthday was December tenth. That made him Sagittarius. And that's like, perfect for a Gemini like me. Gemini and Sagittarius….the party people of the zodiac…we'll be like…

Eddie snapped his fingers. "Are you listening to me, Melanie?"

Melanie shook her head, putting the Rick Martell reveries on hold. "Yes, Max."

"Because I'm giving you a big responsibility here. By helping me to mend this broken statue, you will have helped to repair a broken marriage."

"Oh, Max, I really want to help, but I don't know how to get Jessica out of the store."

"You'll come up with something," said Eddie, handing her one of Max's business cards. "Now remember, this is our little secret. No one, especially not Jessica, must know I was here. In fact, if there are people around me at the shop in Boston, I won't be able to talk freely either. So when you call"—Eddie took back the card and jotted down his own cell number on the back of the Stratton Gallery business card—"you had better use my private number instead."

"Got it."

"You're a smart girl, Melanie. You're going to make some lucky man very, very happy," said Eddie. "I'll need a few hours to get here from Boston, so as soon as you know that Jessica will be gone for at least three to four hours, call me at once."

"Promise!"

"Sweetheart, you're a princess," said Eddie as he headed toward the door. He turned and blew her a kiss. "Our secret!"

Funny, thought Melanie. *That's the second time today that a man has called me a princess, and both times, they were after Jessica.* She sighed as she checked the locks on the back door, then walked to the front room, shut the windows tightly, and switched on the alarm system. As she double-checked the lock on the front door, she felt a surge of optimism.

Everything was going to work out the way it was supposed to be.

Jessica would get back together with Max and move back to Boston. Melanie was going to play a crucial role in making that happen. And Rick? If he really thought of Jessica as more than a friend, he might be a little disappointed at first. But the ocean conservation classes were going to start up in a week. Melanie would be seeing him every day at the beach.

And she'd be wearing her new red bikini too.

The fact that Rick was a Sagittarius was a total bonus. Unfortunately, the file also revealed that he was thirty-eight years old. That was a bummer...he really looked so much younger than that. Melanie had figured he was closer to twenty-eight. If Rick was twenty-eight, that was only a twelve-year age difference which was like nothing. She could work with thirty-eight even though twenty-two years was a stretch. Her mom would be upset, but love happens. What about Elvis and Priscilla? Or that ancient Hollywood guy with Catherine Zeta-Jones...there was like a *hundred* years between those two.

I'm a much better bet for Rick than Jessica. She's gotta be at least 35 years old and married to boot. Not that she's bad for her age—sort of like Michelle Pfeiffer back in "Married to the Mob" or "Witches of Eastwick" days, thought Melanie as she hopped on her bike and pedaled down the driveway. *But honestly, Jessica's gonna be in, like, in menopause before she can give Rick kids.*

Chapter Twenty-Five

Jessica slept fitfully through the night, dreaming of windswept beaches and tempestuous marine storms that pulled her, resisting at first, then resisting no longer, below the crashing waves into a sensuous haven of blue velvet depths.

She awoke, still tired, and went downstairs to make coffee. Under pressure from Nancy, she'd given in and bought a proper espresso machine and, she had to admit, it made the mornings a whole lot nicer. Throwing open the curtains, she looked across the street. The driveway was still empty, but she stared at Rick's cottage so intently that she nearly jumped when the phone rang. Rick! It had to be Rick calling from Canada. Please let it be Rick.

"Yes," she said eagerly.

"Well, hello there," replied a familiar female voice.

"Oh, Nancy. Hi."

"Don't sound so delighted to hear from me!" Nancy chuckled. "Who were you expecting to call you at this hour? Rick Martell?"

"You're turning psychic, Nancy. I guess I was."

"So your little one-on-one beach outing was a success?"

"Melanie told you about that?"

"Yeah, but little Miss 'Live at Five' didn't have any on-the-scene reporters. I take it you had a nice time?"

"Nancy, I don't think it's about having a nice time anymore. At least not for me." Jessica fiddled with the tassel on the belt of her blue silk robe. "Nancy, I think he's wonderful. And I want…I mean I think I want…"

"You think you want what?"

"Him." Jessica whispered the word so low that it sounded like the barest breath of air on a still day. "I want him. I want his arms around me. I know it's awful, but I can't help it."

Nancy burst into laughter. "That's marvelous, honey! You're flesh and blood after all!"

"Nancy, be serious please. I'm serious about this."

"I'm serious too, sweetie." Nancy caught her breath and continued. "And what makes this so grand and glorious is that he's nuts about you too. The only problem was that—with all that hide and seek with the wedding rings—he didn't know if you were free or not. And it was driving him crazy."

"It's still driving me crazy."

"Ah." There was silence on the other end. "I take it that you haven't spoken with Max yet?"

"No," said Jessica miserably. "Because I don't know what possible solution we could come up with."

"I do," said Nancy, "and it's spelled D-I-V-O-R-C-E."

"Maybe so, but I haven't wanted to face that yet."

"I don't think you can put it off any longer," said Nancy gently. "Not if you're starting to think about other men."

"You're right, as usual," Jessica agreed. "I have to talk to Max before I see Rick again. For everybody's sake."

"I wish I could come over and hold your hand while you make that call, but I'm booked solid. Maybe around lunchtime?" Jessica heard Nancy flip through the pages of the oversized agenda book she always carried. "No, sorry. I've got a meeting with a client in Cohasset at two o'clock. By the way, Melanie's running a little late this morning, but I hear the shower upstairs, so she should be over soon."

"Tell her to take her time. I'm not going to open until I talk with Max."

"You'll feel a lot better after you call him," said Nancy. "Trust me."

Nancy hung up, but Jessica kept the receiver in her hand, staring blankly at the wall, until she heard a "phone is off the hook" signal. She pressed a button and listened to the dial tone. The insistent buzzing sounded like a challenge. A dare. She drew a deep breath and dialed the Boston house.

"Hello? Hello? Who's there?"

Eddie's arrogant voice answering her home number at eight o'clock in the morning could only mean one thing. Max and Eddie were living together. She replaced the receiver without saying a word, thankful that there was no caller ID on the Cape Cod landline. She needed to talk to Max, but she could spare herself the indignity of having her message relayed by Eddie.

She shuddered. Even hearing Eddie's voice long distance made her feel depleted, as though his personality had oozed through the telephone cables and tainted the air. She was really obsessing about that creep. Yesterday afternoon, when she got back from the beach, she could have sworn she smelled that nasty, overpowering patchouli aftershave he used.

But that was ridiculous. She looked around, almost as though she expected to see an evil shadow peeking out from behind the bookcase, but Wilder House looked just as cheerful, cozy, and ghost-free as ever. She walked upstairs and got dressed. She'd try Max on his cell later and hope to get him alone.

Wearing neat black jeans and a sky-blue T-shirt, Jessica sat at the cherry wood desk in the front room, balancing the checkbook, when the phone rang.

Please *don't* let it be Rick, she found herself praying silently. Not until I've been able to get things straightened out with Max. She hesitated, then picked up the phone gingerly.

"Wilder House Antiques."

"Jessica, George Ellenbogen here. How're you doing, my girl?"

"George! It's wonderful to hear from you."

Jessica spoke with real pleasure. George Ellenbogen, a retired newspaper executive from Nashua, collected sailboat memorabilia. They ran into each other several times a year at American auctions. Although marine collectibles were not Jessica's specialty, George had offered her good finder fees for locating brass compasses and iron anchors at auction, always paying promptly and generously.

"I got your little note that you'd set up for yourself. Congratulations, my dear, it's about time. I was wondering if you still had that ship's figurehead that you mentioned when we met at that Sotheby's sale last fall."

"Yes indeed." Jessica looked across the room at the thirty-inch high wooden bust of a dark-haired woman wearing a fringed, crimson dress with gold trim.

"Didn't you tell me that it was off the Mary Anastasia, out of Portsmouth in 1869?"

"Yeees," said Jessica slowly as she searched her memory for details on the sale. George Ellenbogen always wanted as much historical data as possible.

"Any details on the past owners?"

"I bought it at the Parkhurst estate sale three years ago, but I'd have to check my records for that. Does that ship have a particular interest for you?"

"I just purchased the captain's log from the maiden voyage, so I'd like to have a piece of the old boat to go with it. I don't suppose you have to check your files for the price."

"No sir." Jessica laughed. "$8,000."

"Hmmm. Steep. Good condition?"

"Near perfect."

"I'm on the road today, but if you can fax me whatever paperwork you've got on it tomorrow, I think we'll have a deal." There was some muffled conversation in the background. "My son's going to be passing through your area tonight on his way back from Wellfleet. All right if he drops by and takes a look at it?" More conversation. "Around eight? Would that be all right?"

Jessica assured him that it would and whooped with joy when she put the phone down. A sale this big didn't come around every day. If she could sell the Mary Anastasia figurehead, she could meet her monthly quota with one fell swoop. Now she had a professional excuse for not opening promptly at eleven. Walk-in customers would be in the way. Finding the files on the Parkhurst sale took priority, and it wasn't going to be a pretty job.

Back in Boston, every sale for Stratton Gallery was neatly cataloged on the computer with its date of purchase, measurements, provenance, condition, and auction history. Jessica knew that because she was the one who did all the drudge work. Unfortunately, she'd never had a chance to treat her treasures with the same formality. "Files" was a euphemistic way to describe the cardboard cartons stuffed with folders, bills of sale, and research that she'd stuck behind the couch when she moved in. She dragged them to the center of the room and dug in.

She opened the first box and began to lay the papers out in a semicircle around her. Yellowing newspaper stories and pages torn from magazines were paperclipped inside auction catalogs. Faded sales receipts were stashed in manilla envelopes, too many of which weren't labeled.

She held up a bill of sale from a small second-hand store in Wilton, New Hampshire. The tiny scrap of paper exuded a bittersweet bouquet of memories. A crisp, sunny autumn day. A long drive through New England hills that sparkled with gold and scarlet foliage. The sharp and sweet taste of apple cider at a roadside stand. Her exultation as she bargained for a carved wooden barber's pole, with traces of the original red and white paint, that she'd spotted in a Vermont garage sale.

Where was that barber's pole now? She looked around the room. There it was, propped up in the corner by the grandfather clock. She leafed through a color brochure from a New York auction house. The first time she'd placed a formal bid there, and bought a pair of decorative sconces, they'd turned out to be infested with wood lice. She'd been furious, but Max had laughed and taken her out to dinner at the Plaza, assuring her that it was all part of the learning process. He'd ordered a bottle of vintage Champagne and told her that…

"What are you doing on the floor with all that trash, Jessica?" Melanie had come in so silently that Jessica, lost in memories of the past, hadn't noticed her arrival.

"Looking for the paperwork from an estate sale I attended three years ago," answered Jessica. "See that figurehead on top of the bookcase over there?"

"You mean the lady in the red dress and the green necklace?"

"I've got a collector who'll pay $8,000 for her if I can find enough historical data on the Mary Anastasia to please him."

"That is super cool," said Melanie, clearly impressed. "Can I help?"

"Why don't you look through that box? We're after a big envelope labeled *Parkhurst*."

"Mom has tons of paper too, all sorts of stuff she can't scan but needs to keep," said Melanie after they'd shuffled through their respective boxes in silence for a few minutes. "She's got them all organized. You need some file cabinets like hers, with hanging folders in different colors."

"File cabinets? That's not a bad idea. I'll look into that."

"You can get some really fantastic office supplies in Boston," said Melanie eagerly. That would get Jessica out of the house for better part of a day.

"They've got big discounts too. Much better prices than you get down here. You should take the day off and drive up to Boston."

"I doubt that the savings on a couple of file cabinets would make up for the mileage and gas. I'll buy something around here." Jessica wiped her hands against her jeans. The dust quotient in the antique business wasn't negligible. "Parkhurst! Got it!" She sat back on her heels and opened the bulging folder. "Heavens, I bought a ton at that sale. Two sets of andirons. One lot of books. Two lots of textiles, mixed. One ship figurehead off the Mary Anastasia, Portsmouth! And look at this. I've got the entire auction history, plus some photocopies from an out-of-print book about the boat." Jessica waved the papers over her head. "Melanie, we've struck gold! You're getting a bonus today!"

"Cool!" cried Melanie. "Way to go, Mary Anastasia!"

Jessica and Melanie were slapping high fives when Rick knocked on the door.

"Hey, ladies. What are you celebrating?"

Melanie turned to Rick with flushed cheeks. "Jessica just made eight grand on an old statue! All because it came off some special ship! How cool is that?"

"That's gotta be pretty cool," agreed Rick, leaning against the door jamb and looking over Melanie's head toward Jessica.

"When did you get back?" Jessica asked.

"A few hours ago. I dropped the cartons off at the Institute so they can start analyzing the samples and uploading the data into the computers. What's been going on here?" Rick's eyes swept over the papers spread across the floor. "It looks like a tornado hit a stationery store."

"It's called a filing system," said Jessica.

"Is it safe to come in?"

"This way." Jessica brushed some papers aside and indicated a path toward the easy chair. "Would you like some coffee or tea?"

"Coffee, if it's no trouble."

"I'll get it," said Melanie. "You too, Jessica?"

"Thanks, Melanie."

"I noticed that you've got the 'closed' sign out front," said Rick as he sat down. "Is this some kind of holiday I forgot about?"

"No, just some paperwork that took priority."

"Well, I'm declaring this a holiday for me. It's my last free day because as soon as the Nova Scotia data is analyzed, I'll be spending day and night at the lab. I thought I'd drive over to Provincetown today. Do you know the town, Jessica?"

"I've worked with some of the art galleries on Commercial Street. That's about it."

"I was thinking more about whale watches."

"Whale watches?"

"Boat trips out of Provincetown harbor. The ecology classes start in a week, and I'd like to check out the group rates and some of the camping options around town."

"Cool," said Melanie as she came in with two brimming mugs of coffee. "I love P'town. Cream and sugar?"

"Cream," said Rick. "Please."

Melanie disappeared into the kitchen.

"Come with me, Jessica. Let's take a day off."

"But the shop…"

"You've just sold $8,000 worth of merchandise. How much more does a self-respecting capitalist mogul need to make in a day?"

"You ought to take Melanie," said Jessica. "She knows the town better than I do."

"*Yes!*" whispered Melanie under her breath. Milk carton and pitcher in hand, she edged closer to the kitchen door to hear better. *A whole day in P'town with Rick Martell? Yes, yes, a thousand times yes!*

"I want to go with you, Jessica," said Rick. "Melanie's got the hometown advantage, but I think we can manage to find the harbor all by ourselves."

Melanie nearly dropped the milk and the pitcher.

"That day at the beach, we started a conversation that we didn't get a chance to finish, and I think…"

A conversation? So all they did at the beach was talk to each other? That was kind of a relief…

"—and I think we're both overdue for a little fun. Have you ever seen a whale up close?"

Jessica stifled a giggle as she thought of Mrs. Braithwaite. "I have to admit, seeing whales hasn't figured on my bucket list," she said drily. "And remember, I'm not exactly a free woman yet."

"You're not free enough to go sightseeing with a friend? We'll have twenty zillion tourists and a pod of ten-ton, ocean-dwelling mammals to chaperone us."

"It's only milk, we don't have cream," said Melanie. She put the small pewter pitcher on the table beside Rick, noticing with a frown that he was holding Jessica's hand much too tightly.

"Milk will be fine. Thank you, Melanie." Rick

reached for the pitcher with his other hand without lowering his gaze from Jessica's face. "I'm trying to persuade your boss to take the day off and help me look around Provincetown."

"Really?" asked Melanie, trying her best to look surprised. "That's cool." Her mind ticked away. This might work in her favor after all because as far as getting Jessica out of the house long enough for Max to do his stuff and win back his wife's affections, Provincetown would work as well as Boston. The important thing was getting Jessica off Rick's radar before they got around to anything hotter and heavier than conversations.

True, Provincetown was a lot closer to Brewster than Boston, but the resort village was so popular that it could take forty minutes for anyone without a residency permit to find a parking spot. "You can get the world's best fried clams on the pier, and there are tons of great shops on the wharf," she said eagerly. *How much time would Max need with the statue?* "And you can't miss the sunset at Race Point," she finished triumphantly. "Everyone goes to the beach and claps. You can't miss that, Jessica, it's, like, super-famous."

"How can I stay until sunset if my client's son is coming by at eight p.m.?" argued Jessica. "And look at this place. It's a disaster area."

"I can straighten it up while you're gone," said Melanie helpfully. *Getting Jessica back with Max—and away from Rick—was well worth a boring afternoon with a bunch of dusty old papers that would be better off in a recycling bin.* "You ought to take a holiday. Enjoy the whales and the boat ride."

"See? All signs point us toward Provincetown,"

said Rick softly.

"I guess they do," said Jessica. She headed to the kitchen and got her bag. Sunglasses, check. A tube of suntan cream—without papaya fragrance—that she'd picked up at the pharmacy yesterday. Check. Cell phone, all juiced. Check. That was probably all she'd need for the day. The Mary Anastasia file was safely stowed atop the dining room table. "Thanks, Melanie. You can take off as soon as you've got all this paper back in the boxes. And you're right about the file cabinets. I'll get on that tomorrow. You've still got the keys?"

"Right here," said Melanie, holding up the keychain. "I used them to get in this morning. Remember?"

"Then let's not keep Moby Dick waiting," Jessica said.

Rick held the door open. "You see, Jessica, everything works out for the best."

It sure does, thought Melanie as she rummaged through the front pocket of her backpack for the engraved business card she'd zipped into it yesterday. Before the jeep was halfway out of the drive, a cell phone was ringing in the back office of an elegant Boston art gallery.

"Stratton Gallery," answered a cool, collected voice.

"Max," said Melanie breathlessly, "the coast is clear."

Chapter Twenty-Six

Why is my mind such a hot mess? Jessica asked herself. *Why can't I be clear about anything at all?* Listening to her inner voice just made things worse. Repeating and repeating itself on an endless loop, it kept nagging her to concentrate on what she truly wanted and to brush all obstacles out of her way.

Big help.

What she *truly wanted* right now was to snuggle up next to Rick Martell, to feel Rick Martell's arms around her, and to run her fingers through Rick Martell's hair. The immediate obstacles in the way of that little scenario were 1) seatbelts, and 2) the gearshift. The bigger and less easily overcome obstacle was her marriage and a job-lot of emotional baggage: a parade of jumbo-sized suitcases crammed with suspicion and distrust, slamming and banging into each other on an endless conveyor belt in her brain.

Cynics said that all men wanted from women was sex. Well, she was just coming out of a marriage with a man who didn't seem at all interested in sex…at least not with her. She glanced at Rick. All he'd ever offered, when you came down to it, was friendship. She only had Nancy's word that Rick was "crazy" about her.

Silence.

Rick kept his eyes directed on the road, as if he expected the asphalt to crumble into dust at any minute.

Jessica fiddled with her watchband, snapping the gold clasp open and shut, deliberately pinching the soft skin on her inner wrist as she stared out the side window. *She'd already made a fool of herself with Max. Was she about to make a fool of herself with Rick? Despite what he'd said at the beach, they weren't exactly equal on the betrayal beat. Sure, he's got an evil ex-girlfriend somewhere in Europe, but I'm married to a guy who's just a few highway exits west. Not that it was much of a marriage, but I've been pretending that reality would go away if I didn't think about it. And if Rick hadn't appeared, I could have gone on not thinking about it. It's easier for him.*

She glanced in his direction, but his profile gave nothing away.

Maybe it's not easier for him. Maybe he's just more honest.

"Rick." Jessica had to clear her throat. "Rick, I'm glad we have this time together." *Dammit. The words sounded so stiff. Like this was a meeting with a client.*

To her surprise, Rick grinned.

"The fair-haired hostage speaks at last. I was beginning to feel like a kidnapper."

"You could have said something."

"An invitation to a whale watch doesn't count?" He rapped his fingers lightly against the steering wheel. "If we're playing by the rules, it's your turn to talk."

Jessica took a deep breath. "I'm married."

"Yes," said Rick.

"I'm not divorced."

"I know."

"Rick, I've got a husband. Doesn't that matter?"

Rick pulled over to the side of the road. The traffic

that rushed by them roared like waves on the beach.

"Where is he?"

"In Boston."

"When and where did you last see him? How did you leave things?"

"A few weeks ago." *In bed with Eddie, but she couldn't make herself say that.* "It's hard to talk about that. I'm sorry."

Rick started the car. "No, I'm sorry for pushing you. But I don't think you love your husband, so I can answer your question. I'm surprised at myself since I'm a fairly conventional man, but this guy in Boston doesn't bother me. What matters to me is you."

Jessica reached for his hand. "You matter to me too."

"That's a start." He shook her hand solemnly. "On the matter of mattering to each other, the vote is unanimous. Now to clear the air before someone slaps a scarlet letter on your jacket which, I understand, is an old New England custom…"

"Rick!" Jessica laughed in spite of herself.

"…I hereby declare that we change the subject and talk about the whales we're going to see. What do you know about whales?"

"They're big."

"Okay, no interruptions. That sign says thirty miles to Provincetown, so at a fact a minute, you'll know just as much as I do by the time we get there."

By the time they parked the car and walked to MacMillan Wharf, the morning whale watch boats had already set sail for Stellwagon Bank. "It's one of the richest feeding grounds in the world," Rick said as he bought tickets for the afternoon cruise. "Which reminds me that I'm hungry. Know anyplace around here?"

"You like Portuguese food?" asked the man behind the ticket desk. "My sister has a restaurant right off Bradford Street. You'll like it."

Twenty minutes later, Rick and Jessica were sitting in front of heaping plates of pasta topped with linguica sausage. Rick was using the paper napkins to sketch silhouettes of humpback, right, and fin-back whales."

"I give up," said Jessica finally. "I've had enough."

"Enough linguica?"

"Enough with the facts about the whales. I'd like a little bit of mystery when I see my first one."

"I get carried away." Rick shuffled through the cruise brochures, then looked at his watch. "Would you be up for a second cruise if the whales don't show on the first one?"

"As long as I'm back at the shop by eight p.m., it's no problem."

Rick gestured for the bill and drank the last drop of the black espresso. "Then let's get going. We've a bit of time, and I wouldn't mind seeing some of the town."

They strolled through town, admiring the rows of gray shingle houses surrounded by emerald-green hydrangea bushes whose flowers resembled explosions of blue fireworks. The tea roses that draped over split rail fences perfumed the air. Rick commented on the frivolously painted yellow, pink, and lavender woodwork on the houses. "That's the Portuguese influence," explained Jessica. "This was a fishing village before it was an artist's retreat. The Blessing of the Fleet every August is famous."

"We'll come back and see it this year," said Rick. "Together."

"Now I'm going to make a rule. Let's not make any plans, okay? Plans make me nervous."

"Plan withdrawn," said Rick. "What's that modern-looking place over there? The one with the big blue sign?"

"Oh, that's a little gallery I used to visit with…" Jessica stopped, flustered.

"They've got a great model ship in the window," said Rick, pretending not to notice her confusion. "I wonder how much they're asking for it?"

"If you're interested in it, let me negotiate the price for you. You've done me so many favors, I'd like to reciprocate." A young man with wavy blond hair was taking down the "out to lunch" sign from the front door as Jessica led the way down the flagstone path. "I've known the owner, Jeff Raleigh, practically forever." In fact, Jeff had always been *quite* flirtatious when they ran into each other at Americana auctions. Maybe she shouldn't be so surprised that Rick was interested in her. Maybe there had been men all along who'd fancied her and she was just too blinkered by Max and her pitiful excuse of a marriage to pick up on their intentions. If she *was* attractive to men, maybe she should take advantage of that.

Maybe this would be a good time to test the waters…

"Jessica, we don't have much time for shopping if we're going to catch that boat."

"We've already got our tickets, and this will only take a minute," Jessica answered over her shoulder. "I used to work with this gallery, and it would be rude for me not to pop in and say hello." She was so new at this idea of being a quasi-single woman. Would it be appropriate to hint to Jeff that she and Max were no longer together? She opened the door. "Jeff, how are you doing…"

She stopped short.

The young man had stepped behind the counter and had his arms wrapped around a distinguished, gray-haired man, kissing him sensually on the lips.

"Oh, not really!" Jessica gasped. Choking, she stumbled backward, knocking Rick into the door jamb, and ran down the path. The two men inside did a double take, and Rick stared at them blankly before he backed out and raced after Jessica. He caught up with her quickly and led her to a bench in front of the Town Hall. Shaking, she lay her head against his shoulder and sobbed silently.

"Jessica, what is it?" he asked as he smoothed her hair gently. "Is there something about that store? Some old memory?"

"It's just that I always thought Jeff had a little crush on *me.*" She fished in her purse for a handkerchief, dried her eyes, and laughed ruefully. "He was always so helpful and gave me such good prices. Of course, I always thought my husband loved me too. I'm such a fool. I honestly thought both of those men were attracted to me. And all of a sudden, I realize that all the men who've shown an interest in me are gay."

"I think you may be forgetting someone," said Rick. "There's me." He lifted her chin gently, winked, and when his lips met hers, it felt like every single siren in the firehouse went off at once. This was so good, so good. In fact, it was nothing like ever before. This was kissing? What had she been thinking a kiss was like before?

"Get a room, you two," said a snide tourist in a Milwaukee T-shirt.

"Flaming heterosexuals," muttered another. "They lower the tone of this town."

The clock tower struck two chimes.

"Oh, the boat!" cried Jessica, jumping to her feet. "The whales!"

"The whales will wait for another day," answered Rick. "Why don't we head back to that restaurant, get you a cup of tea, and go home if that isn't too much planning for you? And maybe we'll have dinner later after your client leaves."

"That would be wonderful, but there's something I have to do first."

"What's that?"

"Apologize to Jeff." Jessica stifled a giggle. "I probably scared him to death."

Rick waited on the curb while Jessica walked down the path to the Raleigh Gallery.

"That was easy," said Jessica when she joined him a few minutes later. "Much less embarrassing than I thought. Jeff thought I was freaked out about that landscape painting that was hanging on the wall behind him. Max wanted it for a special client, but Jeff skunked him with a telephone bid for it at auction last year. I told Jeff it was water under the bridge and that no one at Stratton Gallery held any grudges."

"So all's well that ends well," said Rick, putting his arm around her waist as they walked to the parking lot.

"All in all, Jeff was awfully sweet about everything," said Jessica. "Chris always says that 98.5 percent of the decent men on earth are gay."

"And you know what Mark Twain said?" asked Rick. "There are three kinds of lies. Lies, damned lies, and statistics."

Chapter Twenty-Seven

Melanie paced back and forth anxiously, running to the window every time she heard a car slow down in front of Wilder House. What was keeping this guy? Max had said he was leaving Boston right away, and that was over three hours ago. The more she thought about it, the less she liked this whole setup. Maybe Jessica had good reasons for ditching her husband. Frankly, thought Melanie, if it came to a choice between Max and Rick? Like…no contest.

Besides, what if Jessica came back before the statue was repaired and back in place? Better not think about that one. *What would Mom say if she knew I'd gone behind Jessica's back*? Better not think about that either, Melanie decided.

Where on earth was he?

Finally, a dark blue van pulled into the drive.

"Where have you been, Max?" whispered Melanie as she opened the door. "I've been going crazy."

"I had a little trouble with my credit card at the van rental place." Eddie would have rather done the job right there in Wilder House, but Jimbo, his felony guru, advised against it. If the locks had melted down in the fire, Jimbo reasoned, the job would require heavier hardware than a few little lock picks. "Look, the less we talk, the faster we can get the statue to the repair shop."

"I hope it's not too far away, this repair shop of

yours," said Melanie, biting a nail nervously as she followed Eddie into the house. "I checked the boat schedules and, if they skip the sunset, Jessica could be back by six."

"Just help me get this table out of the way, will ya kid?" Eddie picked up one corner of the display case and gestured to Melanie to get the other side.

"Hey! Wait a second! Shouldn't we take the fragile stuff out of it first? That stuff might get smashed."

"Like you said, kid, time is of the essence. We'll be careful, okay?"

Empty space was at a premium in the front room, so moving the display case away from the statue was like pushing the blocks around in a brainteaser puzzle box. Melanie cried "watch out" every time the contents of the case shifted. When it was out of the way at last, Eddie looked down where it stood and snorted in disgust.

"What's all this stuff doing on the floor?" He glared at the cardboard file boxes that Melanie has shoved under the display case. "Seems like you could have cleaned the place up since you were hanging around on your butt all day."

He tried to kick the first box away with his foot. Too heavy. He knelt on the floor and grunted as he pushed the box across the floorboards.

"C'mon, kid, don't just stand there. Shake a leg."

Max Stratton was sure being stingy with the charm today, thought Melanie. I wonder if he talks like that to Jessica? Maybe that's why she...

"You deaf or something, kid? Get these boxes out of the way."

When the file boxes were flush with the bookcase,

Eddie started rolling the statue to the front door. "Now we're cooking with gas. C'mon, kid, get on the other side and guide a bit. AGGGGH! What the HELL!"

"Max! What did I do? Max?"

"You rolled the thing over my foot, that's all, you idiot!" Luckily, the wheels barely grazed the side of his suede Italian loafer, but it was still painful enough to bring tears to his eyes. Eddie hopped on his other foot and swore under his breath.

"Do you want to sit down for a minute?"

"NO! I just want to get this stupid chunk of firewood OUT of this place and over to the damn REPAIR SHOP as soon as POSSIBLE. That's the plan, right? Making Jessica HAPPY, right? Yup, ease the thing around the corner there. Hey, what's wrong now?"

Lady Hiawatha's left arm, bent stiffly to hold her long-gone cigars, caught on the door frame which left an angry streak of white paint on her polished forearm.

"Max," Melanie squealed again, "she's getting scratched."

"They can fix that up while they're working on the rest. Let's get a move on." Eddie grunted, his face flushed by the unaccustomed physical exertion, as they cautiously—THUMP!—negotiated the front steps—THUMP—keeping their feet well away from the wheels.

"This thing weighs way more than I'd have ever guessed," gasped Melanie. "Jessica sure doesn't have to worry about anyone trying to steal it."

"You'd be surprised," muttered Eddie. "People will steal anything. Get ready for the next step." THUMP! "Only one more to go."

THUMP!

"You climb in the back of the van and hold the head steady while I lift the base," ordered Eddie. He hoped the kid wouldn't notice the hatchet, the crowbar, the chisel, and the power drill that he intended to use on this stupid statue if the lock picks failed.

"We need a building crane or something," said Melanie a few minutes later. With all their combined pushing and pulling efforts, they could raise the statue only a few inches off the ground before their strength gave way.

"You're not trying hard enough," said Eddie, wiping the sweat from his brow. "One, two, three…"

They didn't hear the jeep pull into the drive across the street.

"Rick! Someone's stealing Lady Hiawatha!" Jessica whispered in horror. She reached for her cell phone and dialed 911 which responded instantly. "There's a robbery in progress at Wilder House Antiques, Route 6A. They're putting things in a blue van. No, I won't confront them. Um, I don't know how many robbers there are. Rick, can you see…?"

But Rick had already vaulted out of the car and was running toward the van.

"Max, look out!" shouted Melanie, shrinking back involuntarily as Rick raced toward them with a murderous expression on his face. "Behind you!"

A firm hand whirled Eddie around.

"Hey," said Rick, "what do you think you're doing?"

"Get out of my way, fool," said Eddie, who reached into the van for the crowbar and waved it in Rick's face, "or you'll be sorry."

"Sorry about what?" asked Rick after his deft uppercut tossed Eddie to the ground like a limp rag.

"Oh, Rick, what have you done now?" moaned Melanie, kneeling by Eddie's side. "You've messed everything up! Max only wanted to fix the statue so that Jessica would love him again."

"What?" Rick turned around in protest to Jessica, who was at his side, cellphone in hand. "Does that make any sense to you?"

"Not at all," said Jessica, looking down with bewilderment at the stunned and speechless Eddie.

"You weren't supposed to know anything about it," protested Melanie. "Max wanted it to be a surprise."

"That's not Max. It's his so-called business partner, Eddie Winthrop," Jessica said to Rick over Melanie's head. "I can't imagine what he was doing here."

"He wanted to fix the statue for you," said Melanie miserably. "That's what he told me."

"Well, he won't be telling us much more for a few minutes," said Rick, who took Eddie's pulse with decided distaste. "What's so important about that statue anyway?"

"No idea. Because of all the fire damage and breakage, I don't think she's worth more than a few hundred dollars," said Jessica. "Maybe I have to reassess her value." She turned to look at the statue, but Lady Hiawatha, whose wheels had discovered the driveway's slope down to the highway, was not sticking around for an appraisal. Gliding majestically, she picked up speed down the driveway until she merged with afternoon traffic on Route 6A.

Her first contact with a municipal garbage truck was not pretty.

The garbage truck survived the impact, although Lady Hiawatha's cigar arm snapped off at the elbow and her legs were crushed to splinters. Sprawled across the blacktop, wheels still spinning, she wasn't going anywhere again.

Jessica raced to the crash scene. Rick, apparently delighted to find another practical use for the leather thongs that bound his ponytail, fastened Eddie's wrists tightly behind his back.

"You might have caused a major accident with that thing!" said the truck driver angrily as he alit from the cab to examine his fender. "Junk you're throwing out, you take it to the *dump*, or it goes on the sidewalk on *Thursdays*. Today is *Tuesday*."

"It wasn't junk," said Jessica, looking down at the ruins of her only family heirloom, reduced to intricately carved chunks of mahogany roadkill.

Rick sauntered down the drive to the crash scene. "He tried to make a break for it, but I persuaded him to stick around until the cops show up."

"Let me go!" shouted Eddie, struggling against the coils of garden hose that bound him to the oak tree on the front lawn.

"Jessica," said Melanie reproachfully, "you shouldn't treat your husband like that. Max only wanted to get back together with you."

"For goodness sake, Melanie, what makes you think that's my husband? That's not Max. That's his seedy business partner, Eddie Winthrop."

"But…" Melanie looked at Jessica in dismay. "But, Jessica, he's in love with you, and he knows *everything* about you and the statue."

The driver popped a can of soda and sat down on

the truck's running board. This was turning into quite a good show.

"There must be something to this statue, or what's left of it," said Rick, prodding the statue's base with the toe of his boot. "Is there some kind of panel down there?" He crouched down and pulled a pocketknife from his jeans and ran the blade over the seams. "It's starting to give…whoa!"

"Way to go!" said Melanie in awe as gold and silver coins spilled over the asphalt like a wooden slot machine gone wild. "She's bleeding gold!"

Jessica crouched beside her, picking through the glitter. "That's a Spanish doubloon, seventeenth century, I think. And these are American, late nineteenth century. This looks like an ancient Roman coin. Why, this must be worth a fortune!"

"But whose fortune is it?" asked Rick, picking up one of the coins.

"Mine," groaned Eddie.

The police siren drowned him out. "Detective Earl McMillan," said the officer to Jessica as he stepped out of the car. "Are you the lady who called about a robbery in progress?"

"Yes," said Jessica, standing up and pointing to Eddie. "And that's the culprit."

"So what's all this?" asked the detective, gesturing toward Melanie who, cross-legged on the pavement, was scooping coins out of the statue as if it was a piñata.

"That's what the thief was trying to get away with," answered Rick.

"But what exactly is that thing?" asked Detective McMillan, scratching his head with a ballpoint pen. "Some kind of super-size piggy bank?"

Epilogue

The last rays of the September sun, emitting a faint orange glow but little warmth, filtered through the delicately wattled windowpanes of the front room. Jessica, curled up on the window seat with a floral-patterned blanket tucked around her legs, leafed through a catalog of antique toys from a New York auction house. Occasionally, she slipped a bookmark between the pages to mark something—a toy train set, a Victorian doll's house, a miniature puppet theater—that looked particularly tempting.

She looked up with a smile as Rick, dressed in a heavy flannel work shirt and faded chinos, walked in from the kitchen with two mugs of hot spiced cider.

"What a perfectly splendid idea," Jessica said as he handed her the cup and bent to kiss her. "I've been slowly freezing to death, but I hate to give up sitting in the window seat. I never want this summer to end."

"Winter's not bad as long as you're not cold and lonely." Rick knelt in front of the corner fireplace. "I think it's time for the first fire of the year." He reached for a well-thumbed copy of the *Cape Codder*. "You done with the newspaper?"

"Hours ago," Jessica replied, glancing at her watch. "Oh my God, it's time for Boston Deco in the new afternoon slot!" she added in alarm, rising from her seat and opening the cabinet doors that concealed a flat-screen TV, Rick's main contribution to the Wilder House decor. "Chris called me this morning to remind me not to miss it or else."

"*…and that's the 'must see' exhibition: Nineteenth-century race-course watercolors, at the John Curtin Gallery in Peabody, through November Eighteenth. Now we're headed for scenic Cape Cod where…*"

"Please don't let this be live," said Rick, striking a match and blowing on the flames. "Your friend Chris is okay, but…"

"Shh," said Jessica. "She came and taped this last week while you were at work."

"I like her a whole lot better when I've got some volume control on her."

"Shh!"

"*…following up on one of the most intriguing stories to hit the Boston area this summer. A home-grown Massachusetts mystery that dates back to the turn of the last century, a story that almost brings to mind a plot from a Nancy Drew or Tom Swift book.*" A blue-and-gold picture of coins spilling out the windows of a Gothic mansion with silver letters spelling out "*The Lost Treasure of Briarcrest*" filled the screen.

"Cool graphic," commented Rick as he crossed over to the window seat. Jessica made room and cuddled next to him under the blanket.

"*When Briarcrest, the now legendary Berkshires manor built by railway entrepreneur Christopher Vogel burned to the ground in 1885, the world assumed that the fabled Vogel fortune had been lost forever.*

"*Boston Deco was the first crew on the spot in Brewster, Massachusetts, just hours after the treasure, concealed for more than a century in a cigar store statue given to the estate's gardener...*"

"Great grandfather Robert," she murmured. "He was the caretaker, not the gardener."

"*...came to light when an attempt to steal the statue was foiled by the owner and a courageous neighbor.*"

"The courageous neighbor would be me," said Rick, leaning in for a kiss.

"Shh," said Jessica. "We're getting to the good part."

A photo of Lady Hiawatha appeared behind Chris's face.

"*Jessica Stratton, proprietor of Wilder House Antiques...*"

Jessica made a thumbs-up sign as the Wilder House logo showed on the screen.

"*...inherited the hollowed-out statue, in which a coin collection of rare value was concealed along with several bundles of now worthless stock certificates.*"

"Not entirely useless," commented Rick. "I could have used them to start this fire."

"The artwork on those early certificates is absolutely gorgeous," replied Jessica. "I'm going to frame them and put them on display for twenty dollars apiece."

"*The treasure came to light, quite literally, in the course of a botched robbery masterminded by a rogue antique dealer named Edward Winthrop III, a former associate in the prestigious Stratton Gallery in Boston operated by Jessica Stratton's estranged husband, Maximilian Whitney Stratton.*

"*Jessica Stratton did not press charges but...*"—

Jessica and Rick both booed and hissed as Eddie's disheveled mugshot flashed on the screen—"*this photo was recognized by French Interpol agents in connection with several stolen etchings and two Klimt forgeries that were confiscated at Paris's Charles De Gaulle airport last April. Mr. Winthrop is currently awaiting extradition...*"

"Poor him," said Rick with a satisfied smile as he lowered the volume.

"Rich me," Jessica said. "I know the court said the coin collection that was hidden in the statue was legally mine, but I must say, I'm rather glad that there weren't any surviving Briarcrest relatives to contest that. I'm not sure I could have handled much more conflict."

"Two hundred thousand dollars is a lot of loot," said Rick, running his fingers through his now much shorter hair. The barbershop was his first stop after they returned from Lydia's wedding last month. "And it was pretty handsome of you to donate most of it to the women's center that Lydia's setting up on the reservation."

"Lady Hiawatha thought it was the right thing to do."

"The old girl's more politically correct than I thought she was."

"What's left of her," said Jessica. The collision had smashed most of the statue to toothpicks, but her sculpted mahogany head and shoulders survived and were now mounted on a stand beside the bookshelf. "Oh, no, poor Max," said Jessica, reaching for the remote and raising the sound as her ex-husband's photo flashed on the screen behind Chris.

"*...but a thorough police investigation turned up*

no evidence that Maximilian Stratton had any knowledge of the questionable activities of his associate."

"By the way, how is the gay divorcé doing these days?" asked Rick when Jessica muted the sound.

"Incredibly happy now that he's officially 'out.' Last I heard, he was getting quite serious about a guy who runs a boutique hotel in Palm Springs."

The amicable divorce had gone through quickly, and Max had signed over Wilder House to Jessica. Now her dream house would be her home…forever.

"According to the Supreme Court, Max can marry that guy if he ever decides to settle down again," said Rick. "And, as a matter of fact, the two of us could get married as well."

"Because I'm divorced now?"

"Because you've got all that money," said Rick, kissing her.

"You bet," said Jessica a few minutes later when she caught her breath.

"We've had enough TV," said Rick, lifting her into his arms and heading for the stairs. "I'm making lamb stuffed with spinach and goat cheese tonight, and we've got yesterday's blueberry pie for dessert. Let's go upstairs and work up an appetite."

"Oh yes," said Jessica, not quite sure whether she was approving the dinner menu, an afternoon of mind-blowing sex, or a marriage proposal.

"OH YES!" she said a few minutes later. "YES, YES, YES!"

She had to say it three times because, when she thought about it, all of the three options were…absolutely perfect.

A word about the author...

Corinne LaBalme lives in Paris, but fond memories connect her to the historic enclaves of Brewster and Harwich, Massachusetts. (In her opinion, the Brooks Free Library and the Brewster Ladies' Library make the Top Ten List of "finest places to discover a book" on the planet!) Corinne's articles about European fashion, food, and fabulous destinations have appeared in *The New York Times* "Travel" section, Diversion, La Belle France, and France Revisited; her cozy mystery, *French Ghost*, was published by The Wild Rose Press in early 2022. Catch up with her @corinnelabalme and if you liked this book, don't hesitate to post a review or sign up for her mailing list at https://corinnelabalme.com/

Thank you for purchasing
this publication of The Wild Rose Press, Inc.

For questions or more information
contact us at
info@thewildrosepress.com.

The Wild Rose Press, Inc.
www.thewildrosepress.com